THE SILVER VOICES

The
Silver
Voices

by

John Howard

Swan River Press
Dublin, Ireland
MMXXII

The Silver Voices
by John Howard

Published by
Swan River Press
Dublin, Ireland
December MMXXII

www.swanriverpress.ie
brian@swanriverpress.ie

Cover design by Meggan Kehrli

Set in Garamond by Ken Mackenzie

Paperback Edition
ISBN 978-1-78380-763-5

Swan River Press published
a limited hardback edition of
The Silver Voices in July 2014.

Contents

❧

To Bill Jacob, Joel Lane,
and Mark Valentine

Artist in Residence

The Artist could call nothing in the world his own except for his body and mind (he did not care to use the word "soul") and the possessions he carried with him. When he stepped down onto the platform at Sternbergstadt station, apart from the clothes he was wearing, with his watch and the small change in his pocket, all he owned was a shabby leather wallet containing his papers and a few hundred crowns in banknotes, and an even more battered leather suitcase containing a few more items of clothing, a small number of books, and a wooden box covered in patterned silver (empty). And, of course, the materials of his livelihood: sketchbooks, pencils, pens, brushes, inks, and crayons.

As the train steamed away towards Kronstadt, the Artist stood in the sun and looked up and down the empty platform. Nobody else had got off the train, and it seemed that no-one had climbed on to it either. He wondered, and not for the first time, whether he had chosen Sternbergstadt as his destination or if it had chosen him. All because in the shop he had unrolled that map of Central Europe, closed his eyes and jabbed his finger down at it, stabbing the paper at random, to see where he was to go. The only condition that he had made to himself, before he opened his eyes to see what lay under his finger, was that his journey's end had to be within the Dual Monarchy's wide frontiers. It could have been anywhere from Trieste and the Adriatic coast lying below it in the south to the Ore Mountains of Bohemia or Cracow in the north; from mountainous Vorarlberg in the west to out beyond Lemberg far to the east. He had then bent over the map and, lifting his finger, made out that it had fallen squarely on Sternbergstadt, in Transylvania. At least the Artist had heard of Transylvania. And he had even bought the map, which was now just one more of the many sheets of paper folded up in his suitcase along with his sketchbooks.

The Artist strolled slowly along the platform and towards the station exit. An old man wearing the uniform of the Imperial and Royal State Railways held out his hand, and the Artist surrendered his ticket. The official nodded, and the Artist proceeded on his way, out into the town. Before setting out the Artist had studied the map in his old Baedeker. The station lay on the north side of the quarter known as the New Town, even though most of it dated from the first half of the previous century. As he wandered along in the direction of the centre of Sternbergstadt, the Artist gazed at the gracious early baroque houses, churches, and commercial establishments that lined the street. It was very quiet in the noontime sun. He crossed a square, and soon reached the bridge over the river. The two hills of Sternbergstadt, lapped by houses like the incoming tide, and surrounded by walls, rose up in front of him. The street continued through the old fortified gateway. The great gates themselves had been long removed; as he passed under the heavy gothic arch, the Artist recalled that he was entering the town through Bridge Gate.

A carriage rumbled towards him, and he jumped out of its way, clutching his suitcase to his chest. The driver grinned down at him, and curtains were flicked apart for a moment before closing again. The Artist wandered on through the town. The necessity of finding accommodation could wait for a few hours; he wanted a glass of cool beer, with bread and cheese, and perhaps pickles. He came out onto a large paved open space, which he saw was called Star Square. One side was dominated by a steep hill, its slopes rising above the houses and shops, unbuilt upon except for where a wide flight of steps opened the way to the top. The Artist spotted an inn, the Seven Stars House, and walked through the open door and into the courtyard at the back. Sitting at a table, he put down his suitcase, took off his hat and unbuttoned his jacket. He ordered dark beer, and a plate of warm bread and pungent cheese appeared in front of him. He called for another glass of beer. The Artist ate and drank, refreshing himself after his journey. Now he had truly arrived in Sternbergstadt.

The sun filled the courtyard with a greenish, almost marine light; vines twisted around the wooden pillars supporting the inn's upper floors, and plants in large ceramic bowls or pots dotted the uneven stone-flagged floor. Shadows crawled as the afternoon advanced. The Artist took out a piece of rough paper from his pocket and pressed it flat on the table top. He started sketching, his eyes darting around the courtyard, taking in its features as well as the other customers sitting at their tables. His pencil flew over the paper.

A man got up from his table and walked across to where the Artist was sitting. The Artist had noticed him when he had arrived: a tall, wide-shouldered heavy-set man with abundant white hair and a closely trimmed beard. Dressed entirely in black despite the heat, he had not removed his black hat as he carefully unfolded silver spectacles and consulted the menu as if it had been an illuminated manuscript. The waiter—more likely the proprietor himself, the Artist had thought—had treated him with deference and respect, even as a joke passed between the two men.

"I hope you are not proposing to offer that in lieu of payment," he said. "You would not succeed, I fear. Even though it is rather good, if I may say so."

The Artist looked down and saw that a drawing of his new critic had appeared on the paper.

"In other circumstances I might try that," the Artist replied. "But I have a little money. I can easily pay for my food and drink."

The man picked up the sketch. "Nevertheless, if you would permit me, I will pay the cost of your meal if I may keep this."

The Artist nodded slowly. "Of course. Please." He paused. "Would you like to sit down?"

"Thank you. My name is Anton Petrescu. I do not think that I have seen you here before."

The Artist introduced himself and explained that this was his first visit to Sternbergstadt.

"Have you found somewhere to stay?"

"No, not as yet. Perhaps you could recommend somewhere? It would have to be not expensive, because my funds are strictly limited, at least at the moment."

Petrescu took out his spectacles, put them on, and then took them off again. "This is a decent, respectable place," he said. "But of course you are an artist, you might wish for somewhere rather less—"

The Artist assured Petrescu that respectability had never caused him any difficulties. He said that as long as the inn was generous with the food and it was of good quality, and the beer remained as drinkable as that which he had already consumed, and the accommodation was clean, then the Seven Stars House would be perfectly acceptable. Petrescu called the proprietor over, and all arrangements were swiftly made. Hands were shaken, and a banknote changed hands. Three glasses of fiery schnapps appeared and were empty a moment later.

When the proprietor had gone, Petrescu said, "And now I would like to invite you to dinner this evening, at my house. Quite informal, I assure you. I live in Mediasch Street. Just ask anyone for Lawyer Petrescu's house. They will direct you." He touched his hat and left.

The Artist spent the rest of the afternoon in his room, unpacking and arranging his few clothes and books. He moved the old table to a position under the window, and placed his sketchbooks and drawing materials on it. The room opened out onto the second gallery, and was made cool and shadowy by the overhanging roof and trailing vines. A large brick and stone fireplace revealed that the room should be equally comfortable in winter. Sitting at his new working place, the Artist opened one of his books, a collection of cartoons and verses by Wilhelm Busch, and began to read until it would be time to leave for dinner.

The chambermaid told the Artist how to reach Mediasch Street. Within moments of leaving the inn he forgot most of what she had told him. He crossed Star Square, avoiding the southern side when he discovered that the buildings all seemed to be covered in scaffolding and there was no way through. The Artist wandered along the High Street, and turned off in what he hoped was the right direction as soon as he could, and was soon deep in the maze of the town's narrow streets and lanes. Further enquiries from passersby sent the Artist off in another direction; he could see that the wider, gently curving street led towards the town wall, and another gothic gate seemingly tunnelled through it. On the other side the street continued, unbroken, for a short distance. Then suddenly the Artist found himself standing at the edge of a wide avenue, stretching away on either side. He had strolled along the

Ring in Vienna, and seen photographs of the boulevards of Paris and Regent Street in London. This wide street was still partially under construction: elaborate four and five storey buildings, in a mixture of classical and Italianate styles, alternated with empty spaces full of piles of bricks and cut blocks of stone. Trees had been planted along both sides of the road, and their dusty branches spread over already uneven pavements. The Artist plodded along the length of one extensive building, which began and ended in circular, balconied, projections with small copper-domed roofs. The sign proclaimed the wide street to be Budapest Boulevard. The glaring newness of the blocks—shops on the ground floor, with offices and apartments on the floors above—contrasted with the gentle faded colours and crooked corners of the buildings within the walls.

Soon the Artist reached a large circular space with a fountain in the centre. Several streets converged there, and it was surrounded by tall white buildings with steep tiled roofs. He stopped a fashionably-dressed young man coming out of a shop, who told him it was Paris Circus. Then the Artist asked the way to Lawyer Petrescu's house in Mediasch Street.

"Why do you go to see him? If he had his way, none of this would have been built. I could not meet my friends at the Hotel Paris and smoke and drink plum brandy and talk with them about the wonderful changes that will take place. Sternbergstadt would still just be a medieval backwater town in the back end of beyond of Transylvania at the far end of a dull and complacent Empire. I wish you luck!"

But he told the Artist, accurately, how to find his way to Petrescu's house.

Petrescu was still wearing his black suit and black hat when he opened the door and smilingly bowed the Artist in. Petrescu sat the Artist down in his study, a low and dim room lined with bookcases, pictures, and maps. A glass of red wine appeared on the small delicate table next to him; it was exquisite, and he sipped it gratefully.

"Those new streets are very dusty," the Artist remarked.

"They are horrible, terrible," Petrescu said, pacing up and down the length of the room. He pointed at a map on the wall. "Why, do you know that the plan is to completely encircle the old town with these wide roads, boulevards as they call them? I have tried to put a stop to it, but I cannot. I said to the Town Council, why not just demolish all the walls, and pull down all the towers, and build a road in the shape of a ring just as they did in Vienna? Do you know, my friend, judging from their lack of reaction I think that was what they would have liked to do! But even they didn't have the courage to go that far! Here, a little more wine. Dinner will be ready shortly.

"Now tell me, did you notice this old house? How it is surrounded by streets, yet sits in its own large garden? This was once a small manor house, the one closest to the town walls, and all the land around it was its garden and a farm. Gradually, over the decades and centuries, the land was sold off and built over with pleasant streets and squares, like in our New Town, if you have seen that."

The Artist indicated that he had.

"But the building of Budapest Boulevard and Paris Circus changed all that. I was able to prevent my house and small piece of land from being destroyed. No, Lawyer Petrescu hasn't quite forgotten all that he ever learned in his books! But almost everything else was pulled down and replaced by those monstrosities. And with more to come. Do you know what this quarter is now called? What it says on the new maps? Franz-Josef-Stadt! I ask you! Now I am a loyal subject of His Majesty, even if you might not think so because of my surname, and I do not like to see such destruction linked with our King and Emperor. I am also a loyal Transylvanian and Romanian patriot, and I do not like to see our towns needlessly ruined. But the joke is, they are calling it Parisville. Parisville! That's what it will be known as!" Petrescu strode over to a clock on the mantelpiece, and tapped its glass face as if it were a barometer. "Ah, dinner."

Madame Petrescu served the meal herself, and they ate by candlelight in the low and dark dining-room. Glass and silver glittered and glimmered. Petrescu talked enough for all three of them as the Artist listened politely and Madame Petrescu smiled indulgently and ensured that the courses appeared and the wine glasses remained filled.

"Now tell me this, my friend," Petrescu said. "You already know Star Square, do you not? Where the Seven Stars House is? Did you notice anything about it? Well?"

The Artist considered for a moment.

"Yes, an entire side of the square seemed to be cordoned off, all the buildings covered with scaffolding."

"Yes! Quite! And do you know why?" But Petrescu carried on talking, not waiting for any reply from the Artist. "Another boulevard! Connecting Paris Circus with Star Square! Do you not realise what that means?"

Madame Petrescu leaned over and touched her husband's arm. "Of course he does not know, Anton. He only arrived here this afternoon. You told me so yourself."

"Yes, well, quite . . . What it means, my friend, is that not only will parts of the town inside the walls be demolished this time, but a section of the wall itself as well. It's unheard of! Those walls kept the Mongols out, the Turks out. They kept out all the invaders from the east and from the west. They have never been pierced or destroyed in war. I cannot stop it, but I can make sure that we know what we've lost." Petrescu drained his glass and threw his napkin down on the table. He got up and kissed his wife. "A magnificent meal, as ever, my dear; I don't know how you do it. Now we must leave you."

The Artist followed the old lawyer back into his study. Petrescu produced a dusty bottle of brandy.

"When I saw you sketching, and that drawing of me, I had a great thought. It was as a gift from the Almighty. I will come straight to the point. I want you to draw the areas of the town that are being pulled down and replaced. I want you to draw the walls and streets and squares and houses. I want you to record it all with your pencils and brushes. You will be seen to have breathed life into the vanished past. Now, I can pay you at least what it will cost you to stay at the Seven Stars House, so you can stay in Sternbergstadt for as long as necessary. Come, my friend, what do you say? Your drawings will be displayed in my museum. Oh, I haven't said anything about that, have I? I have decided that my house, this house, shall become the museum of Sternbergstadt for all time."

The Artist decided to walk back to the inn by the same route as before. Under its glaring electric lighting, Budapest Boulevard was crowded with strollers. It seemed to the Artist that the entire population of the town—at least all of it not out of its twenties—must have been promenading along the uneven pavements. Entering the walled town, the Artist found the streets to be virtually deserted. The contrast between Sternbergstadt inside and outside its walls was striking: over the distance of a few tens of metres, a century or more might have passed by. Entering Central Square the Artist saw the dark bulk of Castle Hill rising from the end of a long street, and the soft glow of the white walls and towers of the Castle and the Castle Church in the moonlight. Outside the walls he had not even noticed that the moon was riding high in the sky.

He thought that one of the towers would be a good place to observe the town from and to start to get his bearings.

Early the next morning the Artist walked the length of the High Street and climbed the wide and shallow steps that wound their way up and around the slope of Castle Hill. The gatekeeper explained that the Castle now served as the Town Hall, with most of it being closed up, the heavy furniture in its echoing rooms gathering dust except when the Governor of Transylvania chose to visit. The man was launching into a colourful account of the hour-long visit of the Empress Maria Theresa, as it had been told to him by his grandfather, when the Artist cut him short, mentioning Anton Petrescu's name, and asking if he could be allowed to make the ascent to the top of the highest tower.

The custodian pulled open a drawer and extracted a huge bunch of keys. "So you want to draw the town?" He said. "Well, I suppose Lawyer Petrescu knows what he is doing. He has been a member of the Town Council several times, and was always decent enough to me." He handed the Artist a key. "Here. It's to the Governor's Tower. Cross the courtyard, and go through the archway with the antlers over it. Then go along the corridor, and it's the second door on the left. The key will open it. Then it's upwards all the way. And the best of luck to you!"

The low wooden gallery encircling the top of the tower provided a panoramic view of the town, as well as the countryside beyond, and the distant mountains beyond that. A thin invigorating breeze blew through the wooden arches, increasing the Artist's feeling of having ascended to a changed realm. Surely the air was different up there, and lit through by a different sun in the deep blue above. Looking down for a moment, the Artist saw the steep roofs of the castle falling away far below. Farther out stretched the roofs and chimneys of the town: huddled houses, with their courtyards and secret gardens, were spread out like a patterned blanket roughly thrown over a sleeping body. The bare bulk of Star Hill loomed at the other end of the High Street. Star Square, distorted by height and distance, was visible, as was a wide swathe of destruction leading away from it, cut through streets and houses and leaving a gap like a missing slice of cake. The town was hemmed in by its walls, but the New Town and boulevards spread out over the flat land outside them. The Artist gazed out from his vantage point, fixing landmarks in his memory, and noting down areas to seek out for closer inspection.

Once returned down into the ordinary air of the town, the Artist made his way to Star Square and found an inn hidden away in a blind alley next to the demolition site. Here the men pulling down the buildings to make way for the new boulevard gathered during their short midday break. The Grapes Inn was very different to his own Seven Stars House on the other side of the square, but the beer was good and cheap, and a few crowns soon secured for the Artist the approval and acceptance of his new acquaintances.

"Yes, all these old houses and streets are coming down, we're cutting through them all," one man said, making chopping motions with his arm. "Trieste Boulevard it's going to be called. It'll be the finest street on either side of the mountains. And I know. I've been to Bucharest, once. I tell you, one day when it's all finished I'm going to come back here and stay in that Hotel Paris, and walk along the boulevard in my best suit, smoking a fine cigar, and I'll think that I helped to make all this!" He finished his beer as his workmates burst out laughing. Wiping his mouth, he said, "Mark my words! When we've knocked down that wall, there'll be nothing to stop progress. It's almost the new century. What great changes we'll see!"

11

After his generosity the Artist readily obtained permission to sketch the men at work, and the half-demolished buildings with their façades broken open and floors falling away from the walls. He climbed up precarious piles of rubble and shattered wood, and filled page after page with drawings. He wandered along the top of the town walls until he came to the place where a barrier had been put across the path, where the new boulevard would pass through—too wide, too modern, to permit construction of a bridge to keep the circle of the walkway whole. And the Artist noticed that he was not always alone: he sometimes met a photographer, laboriously checking his equipment, preparing to photograph a particularly artistic ruin before it was removed, or the newly-revealed inner side of the town wall. The two men compared notes, and found that both had been commissioned by Lawyer Petrescu; but agreed that they were not in competition with each other.

From time to time Petrescu joined the Artist as he worked, or as he sat in the Seven Stars House relaxing in the velvet evening with a glass of beer and plate of bread and cheese. He would examine the Artist's drawings, the sheets of paper and sketchbooks spread out on the table between them. Petrescu would nod his approval, and sometimes suggest new viewpoints and angles that the Artist should find and use. As the boulevard advanced, and the wall was finally pierced, the Artist drew every inch of the city. He defined it on paper; more and more paper as the old houses came down and were replaced by the wide paved road lined with tall blocks of apartments, offices, and shops. There were times when he drew in extraordinary close detail, spending hours sketching a gothic window, a balcony, a stretch of polychromatic garden wall dreaming in the sun. And sometimes the Artist wielded his crayons, drawing impressionistic and misty open-air views of the town from the top of Star Hill or the tower of the Lutheran church. Over the days and evenings when Petrescu sat with the Artist, turning over the pages of his sketchbooks, shuffling through his drawings, or studying old and new maps with an almost agitated intensity, he came to feel that Petrescu was somehow coming to terms with the changes being wrought in his city.

On one particular evening the two friends sat sipping plum brandy out on the crooked gallery outside the door to the Artist's room at the Seven Stars House. Soft lamplight threw the shadows of vines on to the white wall behind them; they were in a deep forest contained within the bounds of the streets and buildings all around them. The Artist thought of the harsh electric lights of the boulevards, and the dusty stunted trees, and was glad that he was not among them. And as twilight advanced, once more Petrescu turned his thoughts over in his mind, giving them voice.

"I constantly maintained that with its walls complete the town would always retain *something* which would otherwise be lost if the walls were breached. I do not mean expansion, change, progress, all those things—they cannot be stopped and one should not try—I mean the *essence* of the town, if I can express it that way. But does that depend on walls to keep it in? Does that also therefore mean that something is kept out? And if so, what? Some sort of 'impurity'? I do not like that. The physical and psychical aspects of the town are complementary, but one cannot rule the other. Short of total obliteration perhaps the essence will survive and work on native-born inhabitants, immigrants, visitors—all who love and appreciate the town, whether they know it as Sternbergstadt or Steaua de Munte. Anyone who refreshes themselves in body and spirit here, who takes from this blessed town, but above all gives something of themselves to it for the present and future: they are the true walls which will ensure the town's uniqueness, essence, and its survival."

Lying in bed after Petrescu had gone home, the Artist deliberated on what his friend had said. Perhaps his time in Sternbergstadt was moving towards its end. To be sure, the newspapers were still full of the plans to complete the construction of the ring of boulevards embracing the town outside its walls. And the course of the walls was not completely secure: a vast new space to be called Empress Elisabeth Square was being laid out between Budapest Boulevard and Star Hill, and a long stretch of the wall was due to be pulled down to accommodate one side of it. An occasional editorial in one of the town's newspapers still called for the demolition of the walls entirely. But the Artist thought about the sense of equanimity that Petrescu had started to demonstrate earlier. It certainly had not been due to the plum brandy . . .

A couple of days later, the Artist was strolling along the top of the town wall below Castle Hill. The river curved around the base of the hill, and the wall fell away in a sheer drop to the river. As he walked, people sometimes nodded and smiled at him: the Artist had become very well-known to many of Sternbergstadt's inhabitants as he wandered about the town, stopping here and there to take out his sketchbook or a scrap of paper and try to capture what he had seen. But now, for once, he was not carrying a sketchbook. He strolled back and forth along the curving pathway, looking up at the steep slope of the hill, capped with its castle, or down into the swiftly rushing river below. The Artist was leaning on the parapet, munching a roll he had saved from his breakfast, when he noticed that someone was standing next to him. It was Petrescu.

"I have been hunting around the town for you," he said, slightly out of breath. "I want to ask you something. I'll come straight out with it. I offer you here and now the position of Curator of the new Sternbergstadt Town Museum." Petrescu named a regular remuneration that surprised the Artist with its unexpected but characteristic generosity. "I want to make it clear that you would still have plenty of time in which to pursue your artistic work. In fact you will be able to use most of your time in any way you wish. What do you say?"

At dinner that evening, the Artist informed the proprietor of the Seven Stars House that he would be starting to look for a small house of his own in the Old Town, and would then no longer require his room at the inn. The proprietor said that he did not need to rush into anything. There were many other and finer rooms available in the Seven Stars House. As the proprietor later observed to his wife, their guest had long ago become a member of the family.

Boundaries

When I was eventually demobilised in 1919 I returned to the position in the family business that I had left nearly five years before. I soon resumed travelling throughout Central and Eastern Europe, trying to re-establish old contacts and make new ones. I spent much time in negotiating the sale of our products, and in seeking potential new agents in the major cities of the region. There was a great deal of work to be done. The break-up of the Austro-Hungarian Empire, and all the new and redrawn frontiers that now snaked across the map—the results of the numerous treaties following in the wake of Versailles—had done great harm to the economic unity of the Danube area and beyond. The delicate balances of trade, which had only been achieved, slowly and ponderously, over the previous decades if not centuries, had been seriously damaged. The life-giving stream of commerce needed to flow smoothly once again, and the company was depending on me to play my part. And that was something I had never turned away from, no matter what the situation.

On the occasion that I am going to describe, I had travelled the short distance from Vienna to Prague. In Vienna I had been filled with sadness for what had been lost. Only two years before it had been an imperial capital; but Vienna was now merely the oversized head atop the tiny, shrunken, and ailing body that was the new Austria. So it was with a sense of relief that I journeyed across yet another new frontier into what I still thought of as Bohemia, but which I had to learn to call Czechoslovakia. As with Vienna, the war had left Prague unaffected physically; psychically was a different matter. The contrast could not have been more complete: in Prague a liveliness and vitality filled the air. Prague was now the capital of an independent state once again, and the crowds in the streets seemed to feel that old President Masaryk, high in his castle of Hradčany, symbolised, perhaps rather oddly, a new and young country with much to do and still more that it wished to do: a country that was going places. And the business possibilities would be, hopefully, tremendous.

But that was not all. On the other side of the ledger there were the grievous losses of the youth and mature manhood of the nation, which the recent exploits of the Czech Legion far to the east, fast becoming legendary, did not quite make up for. And there were still many, whether Czech, German-Austrian, or one of the other nationalities, who even then still looked back to the days of the Dual Monarchy with nostalgia and regret. The blank areas on numerous walls, left by the removed portraits of Franz Josef or Karl, seemed to summon up the feeling there was indeed something missing, even amidst all the bustling practicalities and evidence of hard work going on all around Prague.

I was staring at such an empty space on the wall in the large, low, and dimly-lit hotel restaurant where we had just sat down. I remembered the room from years before, crowded with stolid Habsburg civil servants eating lunch, drinking beer, and discussing the political complexities of the day. Nevertheless, I was in a very positive mood, as I had just signed an agreement to considerably expand our agency in Prague. A good luncheon at least was called for, with perhaps a fine dinner that evening, and drink, and entertainment. I was shaken out of my reverie by a light pressure on my forearm. My companion, sitting opposite me—it was James Shaw, a sensible young man even then, and who did well for himself and now manages our Toronto office—had leant forward to rouse me from my thoughts.

He inclined his head almost imperceptibly. "You're under observation."

Before I could turn round and see for myself, a shadow passed me, and a man sat down at our table, next to Shaw. Smiling, he nodded at us both, removed his hat, raised his arm and snapped his fingers.

"Another beer each, gentlemen, yes? Dark beer, I think?"

I was too surprised to react immediately. I had heard stories of such brash behaviour passed on from our representatives travelling in the United States; some of them retailed by Shaw himself, who had been there. It was not meant to be rude or disrespectful, I had been assured, but if that was the direction in which business was moving in the New World, I for one preferred the commercial practices and courtesies still to be found in Old Europe.

A foaming glass of beer appeared on the table in front of each of us, including our surprise guest (or did he think I was his, I wondered?) who lifted his glass in an unmistakeable toast.

"Gentlemen, your health!"

I raised my glass and drank. Shaw drank also and put his glass down, wiping his mouth with a napkin. He raised an eyebrow. I knew that meant that he wanted to know what was happening, but that he would tactfully plead another appointment or other reason to make his departure and leave me alone if I so wished. I shook my head in what I hoped was also a similarly subtle manner. I now knew that I was committed.

"Thank you, Mister . . . " I hesitated. By now his features were beginning to look slightly familiar to me. Perhaps he was one of the many people I had shaken hands with over the last few weeks in one of any number of offices, factories, restaurants, or beer-halls. But Shaw, who had been with me for most of the trip, showed no sign of recognition.

"You do not quite remember? No?" He drank again. "I did not wish to intrude, but I see you sitting there, yes, sitting here in Prague, and I think to myself that this is an opportunity that will never repeat again. And I think that we are now perhaps all, how do you say, pieces of flotsam and jetsam washed ashore here, by the recent conflict?"

"You must forgive me," I said. "I have been working very hard, and I do not fully recall . . . " I drank some more beer. It was truly excellent, the way I remembered it from before the "recent conflict". I tried to study the man opposite, but without staring too much. It was all so unexpected.

"I will put you out of your misery, Captain Williams," he said, laughing. "Or I suppose it is Mister Williams now?"

"You know my name. Yes, I do think I remember having met you before, but how and where? I'm still not sure . . . "

"Do you remember Sternbergstadt? Or Steaua de Munte as one has to call it now. Summer 1917, in Stern-bergstadt, Transylvania."

And then it all came back to me. Of course I'd never forgotten my time in Transylvania, then in Hungary and now part of a greatly expanded Romania. It was probably the only part of the war that I would not choose entirely to forget, if I should ever have the choice. Romania had had a good war, eventually. As I had done, even including what I always spoke of as my "escapade" in Transylvania—which if I spoke of it at all, which was seldom, was in a prepared and well-rehearsed version.

My unexpected guest, who seemed to remember so much about me, was Hauptmann Friedrich Michaelis, once (I presumed) of the Imperial and Royal Army, stationed in Sternbergstadt—and my one-time jailer.

❦

Michaelis laughed again and held out his hand. "Surely we are no longer enemies?" he said. "You have had a good war. The tables have been turned. I am the one who has possibly lost my country, everything. In any case, our dear old Europe has changed beyond all recognition. Do you not agree? Come, please."

I stretched out my hand, and we shook. He also shook hands with Shaw, who had been keeping a most admirable and uncharacteristic silence. Here were two former enemies, now no longer enemies, even if certainly not friends. But we did have an aspect of a shared past, that much in common: he played an intimate part in my Transylvanian 'escapade'. Although we were caught in the middle of war, we had managed to create something else above and beyond it, something that had briefly brought together soldiers fighting on two different sides, even if temporarily not in combat, but still in a state of war, and which put that aside even as another contest took place between us. Far from home, detained against our will, I had helped to create a corner of England, to bring it to life deep in the country of our enemies. When it was all over, we had naturally still parted as enemies, but ones who had shared much, and could perhaps appreciate what the values of our deeds could offer. They were values that would now be needed in the new and frontier-ridden Europe, where old values were largely meaningless, more than ever before. Michaelis and I had been captains of opposing forces, and while involuntarily together had captained opposite teams, in what was surely the first cricket match ever to have been played in Transylvania.

More beer appeared in front of us, as if by magic. There was a small bottle of schnapps, too. A waiter was now hovering close by with menus. "I would be honoured if you would allow me . . . " Michaelis said, as he beckoned to the waiter. "They know me well here. I can recommend—" He spoke to the waiter in a rapid flow of German, switching at the end to Czech and a little Magyar. The waiter nodded and obediently wrote Michaelis's order on his pad. They exchanged a joke and the waiter went away smiling.

"We will make a fine meal, gentlemen," Michaelis said. "I sense you are festive."

"Yes, we have concluded our immediate business in Prague satisfactorily, sir," Shaw answered. He looked at me for confirmation.

"I think I can allow Mr. Shaw to say that much," I said. But I did not want to talk of commercial matters, especially with someone who, for all I knew, could be a rival. "Where are you living now?" I asked.

"Beautifully played and deflected, Williams!" Michaelis laughed. "With all the skill I remember from Sternbergstadt! However, to make an answer, I am living here in Prague. There are members of my family in many cities, and so it was not difficult to find a place here. As I possibly hinted earlier, I have very probably lost my country, now that Transylvania is joined to Romania and my home town's very name is changed. Perhaps I might never be able to return to the house in which I was born." Michaelis drank more of his beer and poured out schnapps into tiny glasses. He drank that too.

I played for time, but felt it was running out. One cannot travel in the company of a man like Shaw for several weeks without revealing something of one's self and

21

gaining confidences in return. So I knew all about Shaw's family, his literary likes and dislikes, which music-hall artistes he is passionate about at any time, and the latest and best models of motor car being developed and produced in England and the United States. And Shaw now knew about my school days, my early commercial career with the firm, and my good war. Or most of the story, anyway: he would not have heard about Transylvania from me.

"I would like to remember on happier times," Michaelis said. "For me at least, if I may be permitted to be a little selfish. And I do not recall that you were always so unhappy in your situation with us." He looked around the large and dim room. "Does this not remind you of that hotel in Mediasch? We made a fine lunch there, under the circumstances, I think."

The soup arrived. I had no idea of what Michaelis had ordered for us, but I was hungry now and the smell made my mouth water. The soup was hot and spicy. We started eating.

Shaw spoke out. "Mr. Williams, what does Captain Michaelis mean? I know you like telling a good story. How did you know each other during the war? And what happened?"

"It's a story that should be quickly told," I said, with some irritation. "I knew Captain Michaelis because I was a prisoner in the war for a while. In Transylvania. The captain had been ordered to look after our interests. Given the circumstances, he acted as a gentleman and soldier should." I nodded at Michaelis. "I certainly never expected to ever meet him again. And that is it."

Of course, that was not it. I had never told the full story of how I and two colleagues had ended up in detention in Transylvania, and what had happened there. The story given out for public consumption was that I had been leading a military mission to our new Romanian allies in the autumn of 1916. The invasion had followed so quickly that the mission did not have time to escape, and so we were captured. That was all true.

Michaelis started to laugh. "I like the way you say 'That is it.' That was only the half of it, as you would say, was it not? I know why you were really in Romania. Why not tell your Mr. Shaw the true story? What harm can it do now?"

I drank more beer and finished my soup. I felt relaxed. Maybe Michaelis was right. The war was over. The spoils had been divided. There was a new European order now.

"I'd be very interested to hear about it," Shaw said.

❧

"Very well," I said. "But first a little necessary background. Michaelis will no doubt be familiar with most of it." I looked at him.

"*Ja.*"

I turned my attention back to Shaw. "We must always lay the best foundations we can. The Romanian Royal Family, then. What is their surname?"

Shaw looked puzzled. "I'm afraid I don't know."

"It was, and is, Hohenzollern-Sigmaringen. I take it at least part of that surname is familiar?"

"Yes. Kaiser Wilhelm of Germany was a Hohenzollern."

I nodded. "Quite so. I fear this will become quite a history lesson. When Wallachia and Moldavia were united sixty years or so ago, their first ruling prince was a native Romanian. For numerous reasons, he was soon deposed, and, as was the custom, a member of a foreign noble family was offered the crown. At that time there were plenty of suitable German families to go round. Greece and Bulgaria received German rulers as well. Politicians and the nobility wanted

23

to ensure the neutrality of the Crown, which they could only achieve by not appointing one of their own. The common people were not, of course, consulted. On the whole, these sorts of arrangements worked remarkably well."

Michaelis looked at me, eyes twinkling. "I am certain that Mr. Shaw will profit by your explanation. Come, continue please."

"Well, in the case of Romania, one of the lesser branches of the Kaiser's family was offered the crown. Prince Karl accepted it, and eventually became King Carol I of Romania. He was the uncle of the current king, Ferdinand. As you might expect, as someone related to heaven knows how many German and Austrian rulers, he was rather pro-German. Even though the main influences on Romanian culture were French, the Royal Family leaned towards Germany. The country had been allied with Austria-Hungary and Germany for decades."

"You have visited Bucharest?" Michaelis said, presumably more to Shaw than to me. Of course, I had been there. "It is known as 'Little Paris'. The new boulevards and great buildings are very attractive."

I continued. "When war broke out in 1914, King Carol wanted Romania to fulfil its treaty obligations and join the Central Powers, along with Bulgaria and Turkey. The politicians prevailed on him not to join, and managed to get neutrality declared. It is said that the shock of this caused Carol's death only a few months later. The new King, Ferdinand, was married to an English princess—"

"Oh yes, Queen Marie!" exclaimed Shaw. "She is very popular, I believe. They say the people love her. And she is certainly a beautiful woman! If you read the stories about—"

"Yes, she has the reputation of exercising much power behind the scenes," I said drily. "Queen Marie is credited with influencing Romania to join the Allies and declare war against the Central Powers in 1916. It is said that the Kaiser himself erased Ferdinand from the roll of names of members of the House of Hohenzollern."

Michaelis snorted. "Prussian upstarts!"

"Anyway, the declaration of war was a calamitous error. Romania was unprepared. The Romanian forces gained a few fleeting victories, but the armies of Falkenhayn and Mackensen counterattacked and invaded, overrunning almost the entire country in a couple of months. Bucharest was occupied, and the oil wells at Ploieşti were set on fire. The Government and Royal Family fled to Iaşi." I drank more beer. Another full glass appeared in front of me. "I witnessed it all. However, my colleagues Bradley, Mitchell, and I were not so lucky, and did not escape in time. Ah, here is our main course. I wonder what Captain Michaelis ordered?"

In between mouthfuls, Michaelis talked as I concentrated on the first-rate food. "You are so infuriating, Williams! You cannot come to the point! That can be such an English character trait, I believe." He poured schnapps into our glasses from the bottle that he had ordered the waiter to leave behind. "You were the leader of a special group that had been charged with contacting and maintaining contact with pro-Allied members of the Romanian Royal Family, government, industry, the press, in fact anyone you could influence against us. That is true, yes? Your documents stated that you were part of a military mission, hurriedly sent to Romania to inspect and make recommendations about the improvement of roads and bridges. Your education and training were suitable for that. But your secret diplomacy, in which you influenced the Queen against her husband's own fatherland . . . "

"I did not have to try too hard," I said. "The King was full of doubts about both sides. I think he would have preferred to remain neutral. But you are wrong about his fatherland. From the day he accepted the invitation to become Crown Prince, Romania was his fatherland. He wanted Romania to be in the most advantageous position when peace finally came. In the end I rather think he succeeded, don't you?"

Michaelis did not reply. Shaw was looking at me in a way I hadn't seen him do before. He spoke with a slightly breathless hush that I had never heard before, either.

"You were a spy, Mr. Williams! Now I know why you hardly ever spoke about your war . . . "

"I was not a spy," I said sharply. "I merely had a task to achieve beyond the mission that was generally recognised. We faced three possibilities. I had to ensure that the best was achieved." I picked up my schnapps glass then slammed it down. *Thud.* "One: Romania should join the Allies." *Thud.* "Two: failing that, she should remain neutral, and certainly deny our enemies use of her oilfields." *Thud.* "Three: Romania should never join the Central Powers." *Thud.*

"You could have been shot," Michaelis said. "That winter in Bucharest, after we apprehended you and your colleagues. It was absurdly easy to find out your real reason for being in Romania."

"So why didn't you have us shot?"

Michaelis's face turned into a mask of shock and surprise. "Do you really not know? Could you really not guess? For one thing, your colleague Mr. Mitchell—he was a distant relative of mine. Yes, his surname had been changed slightly, and his family's long residence in your country had moulded his attitudes. But I was familiar with all the many branches of the family. Even if he knew nothing of me, I knew about him. As such, I felt that my duty was to protect him and his companions as far as possible within my power, whether I received gratitude for it or not. Blood, no matter how diffuse, is of the essence. And the other thing, my dear Williams, of course, is that I wanted to give you a sporting chance."

❧

We had finished our meal and were sipping brandy—a local smooth apricot brandy that contrasted with all the fiery schnapps and the mellow, rich dark beer we had consumed. Michaelis said that the finest coffee in Bohemia would also shortly appear.

"Sir, did you mean what you said, about giving them a sporting chance?" Shaw asked Michaelis.

"Yes, I did." He paused. "Although I also felt that it was right to find out as much as possible from them, our involuntary guests. As I said, Mr. Shaw, Bucharest is rightly called Little Paris. But it was a freezing, dark, hungry Bucharest that we were in. Not like Paris at all. I thought of my estate on the other side of the mountains in Transylvania, the lovely manor house of my family, and our fine town house in Sternbergstadt. And there was an internment camp near to the town. Upon Captain Williams's word of honour that neither he nor his two colleagues would escape, I took them under conduct to my home town. It was still cold, but it was better than Bucharest."

I nodded, I hope not too ungraciously. "After occupied Bucharest and the internment camp, Captain Michaelis's house was a very pleasant place indeed. Even before we fled I had heard rumours about the terrible casualties inflicted on the Romanian army, and the conditions that prisoners were being held in. I did not want to share their lot. At heart I was an engineer, a creator—not a soldier or diplomat, who can so often be destroyers. I was glad of our chance to go to Transylvania, and I don't mind admitting it.

"The passage through the Carpathians was difficult. The roads were treacherous, and made all the worse by the huge amount of military traffic streaming against us. But as we entered Transylvania the weather improved, and my first glimpse of it took my breath away. I saw the distant plains far below, like a small and bright painting, lit up by the low sun, frosty and magnificent in the early morning chill under a tall dark blue sky. In the late afternoon that same day we arrived in Sternbergstadt. We had been able to see it from quite a distance. Captain Michaelis pointed it out. In the dusk haze I saw the two domed hills, one crowned with a castle and church, and the other empty. The hills were surrounded by serried rows of roofs, packed on top of each other, and flooding upwards towards the tops of the hills. Smoke rose vertically from the chimneys, and windows glimmered. The war seemed to have been on another continent. Yes, Sternbergstadt was a lovely city, untouched by time or violence.

"After numerous formalities we drove on up the cobbled main street, until we stopped at the corner of a large square, which I guessed to be in the dip between the hills, almost equidistant from them. The front door of a lovely baroque house on the corner opened, spilling light into the darkening square, and two servants approached the car. Why they were not serving in the army I did now know, but I didn't say anything."

Michaelis smiled, and continued. "Yes, we knew how to observe the old Middle European courtesies. I showed you to your rooms, stressing again that upon your words as gentlemen you would not attempt to escape or cause any sort of mischief. Otherwise—well, the internment camp at Weissbach was not too far away. You gentlemen ate a hearty meal, and retired to your rooms. I thanked my gods that I was safely back at home again, in my beautiful quiet town and amongst my people. Justifying my request to keep you out of the camp could wait until the next day."

"And that next day was sunny and cold," I said. "We were shown around the sights, with an old Baedeker for guidance. The Castle, the churches, the Clock Tower, the city walls with their seven red gates: we saw them all. Michaelis was the perfect cicerone. He called us his *Prominenten*, his famous visitors.

"The weeks went by. Sometimes the weather was appalling, sometimes wonderful. But none of us ever gave anything away. Did we, Michaelis? Yes, you were a gracious host, and not just to your relative. But you were our captor. We hadn't asked for special treatment. Part of me felt extremely guilty, especially when we heard stories about the internment camp. Young Charles Bradley, and he was young, felt even more guilty than I did, and took to spending most of his time in the Castle Church on the hill, or in the Roman Catholic chapel. He was always talking to their pastors or priests. He couldn't accept our good fortune. I don't know what the clergy told him, but it didn't seem to do much good. He just retreated into himself. When he wasn't praying he ran around the top of the city walls, or circuits of a playing field on the other side of the river. He had been a keen sportsman at Oxford, a Blue, and was a member of the Leander Club and the MCC."

"He didn't try to get away?" said Shaw.

Michaelis shook his head. "Absolutely not. He had given his word of honour. An Englishman's word is his bond, not so, Mr. Williams? And the townspeople looked out for him. Mr. Bradley was no trouble. Everyone thought he was simply mad. English: of course! At that time he seemed to exemplify why we were winning the war." He drank more apricot brandy. "At least we were winning it in the east, then."

"You indulged all three of us, but especially young Bradley. But you gained nothing. Not even when spring came and he had his cricket idea." I sipped at my brandy. Although I was not (and am not now, for that matter) given to flights of fancy, the end of the long winter released something in what it is convenient to call my soul. The lengthening days and warmer weather were unutterably welcome. "Bradley had continued his running and exercising all through the winter, and into the spring. But one day he vanished. Michaelis came to me in a rage."

"Yes, that is true. I thought that the gentle Mr. Bradley had made an escape. My man saw him running around the playing field, as usual, but when he looked again, there was no sign of him. I am afraid that I rather took my annoyance out on you and Mr. Mitchell. After all, I had no wish to fail and be sent to Ukraine. But he reappeared that evening, tired, dirty, and angry. It turned out he had run all the way to the camp at Weissbach and back again."

I remembered it well. Bradley was incensed. He had talked his way into the internment camp, and seen the bad conditions there. He said that the men were pale and listless, with nothing to do. I replied that at least the winter was over, and they weren't being used as workers on the land or the roads. But in short, I said that I felt it was none of our business. After all, our position was always precarious. But Bradley insisted that we must do something, even if it was only putting a library together for them or organising sports. He kept saying that a healthy mind needs a healthy body.

"Mitchell suggested that we could try to organise rugby teams," I said. "Now that made me think! Rugby. There's a game. I had played a lot of rugby at university, and was still quite fit. And invoking my Welsh origins, admittedly distant, appealed to me. But Bradley shook his head. He said that rugby was not suitable for men in the state that the inmates were in."

"What did he suggest?" said Shaw.

"Why, cricket, naturally," Michaelis broke in. "That most English of games, I think. When they came to me with the suggestion, I could not see any reason not to agree to it. The internment authorities would be pleased that the inmates receive diversion. There would be all the time we needed for a long game. I easily secured permission, subject to promises of good conduct and with the appropriate safeguards."

"Yes, cricket . . . " I said. "Bradley painted me a picture of a long and leisurely game that would build up the teams' strengths rather than test it to possible destruction. He convinced me. But I have to say that I was rather surprised at how readily you agreed."

"Mr. Williams, I considered it to be to my advantage. How could it not be? I thought of you as my *Prominenten*. Perhaps you mad and eccentric English, with your mad and eccentric game, would turn everyone else against you, all those different nationalities in the camp, and perhaps you would turn against each other. I remember that you were not enthusiastic about cricket, as well."

I admitted as much.

"So, then." Michaelis looked around the now quiet room. "I thought that perhaps, as well as giving you amusement and the chance to be good to others, as you so often wish to do, you would get your sporting chance, as I put it. I would test your sense of fair play. And I would benefit by having helped you. You would be under an obligation to me."

"I did wonder at your motives. But Bradley and Mitchell were enthusiastic, and I wasn't going to stand in their way. And I was getting bored with wandering the streets of Sternbergstadt over and over again, picturesque as they were, and reading the same books and magazines over and over again. So Bradley and Michaelis went out to the internment camp and made the necessary arrangements. Of course I agreed to take part as well, but I had no wish to be involved in the selection of the teams and securing the necessary equipment. I left them to it."

"It must've been difficult to get everything right," said Shaw.

"Well, even Michaelis here couldn't pull all the strings. But the detainees responded with enthusiasm. As I recall, there were only tennis balls, and they were almost worn out. And cricket whites were out of the question. By altering uniforms and being creative with such civilian clothing as we could find, Bradley and Mitchell were able to get two teams kitted out so that they were recognisably different. There was a joiner who made stumps and bails, after Bradley had drawn a diagram for him. I found an old ledger suitable for a score book. But the hardest item to find was also just about the most important: a cricket bat."

I was now growing decidedly mellow. It seemed to me that as well as the fine meal, we had all consumed a considerable amount of beer, brandy, and other beverages. I was beginning to find some pleasure in recalling aspects of my time in Transylvania.

Shaw's expression grew serious. "One couldn't play a decent game at all without a proper cricket bat," he said. "If there wasn't one to be found . . . "

"Yes," said Michaelis. "Bradley and Mitchell seemed to feel about that the way you do. Once Mitchell came to me and said he was all for calling the game off. But I could not allow that. I suggested that the carpenter, who had made the wickets, also make some bats." Michaelis sipped his brandy and laughed softly to himself. "One would have thought that I was asking for a plan to stop the war within a day, and with all combatants satisfied. Apparently making cricket bats out of the wood available, in the time required, and by an untrained man, was all completely out of the question. I suggested to Bradley and Mitchell that they at least draw a bat, and try to get two or three made. But they were adamant. It would not be possible, they said, like trying to explain colour to someone blind from birth.

"Then I had an inspiration. Through the military postal system I contacted an old school friend who was in the War Ministry in Vienna. I thought that if a cricket bat could not be found in that city, then one was not to be found anywhere in the Empire.

"My friend thought I was crazy, but he persevered. And a few days later I received a long and heavy package, brought by one of the internment camp guards, to where it had been delivered by courier along with other, more official, objects."

I took up the story. "Yes, as Bradley and Mitchell were throwing tennis balls around on the playing field, Michaelis summoned me to see what he had received. The box from Vienna contained three cricket bats. Two were well-used, and one was absolutely new. Michaelis showed me a letter. Under a diplomatic pretext his friend had entered the sealed British Embassy in Vienna, and searched the living quarters of the younger diplomatic staff until he found what I wanted, left behind in 1914. My colleagues were overjoyed when I presented them with the bats. And I told them to be careful, as they would have to be accounted for after the war."

"So you were able to get teams together and play the match?" asked Shaw.

"Certainly," Michaelis said. "Williams here explained the rules and taught me to score, and I kept the score. Bradley was the umpire. Williams and Mitchell played for a team of *Prominenten* assembled from the camp, against another team of less-exalted inmates. A few of the Commandant's personnel were also assigned to each team, to spice things up, I think you might say. Part of the playing field outside the walls was prepared, and the game took place over five days in the July of 1917. Very few of the townspeople took any interest. In fact, the only spectators were the internment camp guards, who were also doing their duty."

"It all passed off remarkably well," I said. "It was like those football matches on Christmas Day 1914 at the Western Front, with all sides showing forbearance and goodwill." I picked up my glass and tipped it towards Michaelis. "Nothing of what you were hoping to happen actually happened, did it? The teams played the game. There was no dissention or rivalry. Somehow the real old spirit of the game prevailed over us all. Perhaps it was because there was fighting and struggle enough outside of our quiet corner of Transylvania. I don't know. I think that we all realised that there would still be numerous opportunities in the future, both welcome and unwelcome, to have enemies and fight them. But in that open landscape, under the walls of Sternbergstadt, below its hills and towers slumbering in the warm sun, we wanted something different. And that's the way it was."

"And after it all ended you went your separate ways . . . " Shaw mused.

Suddenly Michaelis snapped his fingers and a waiter scurried across to our table. "If you please, the bill."

I reached for my wallet, but Michaelis shook his head. "You are my guests. I am your host this time, not your jailer, I hope! I will pay. It is my chance. Maybe we will meet again." He stood up, and clicked his heels almost imperceptibly. "Mr. Shaw. Captain Williams." He thrust several banknotes into the waiter's hand as he strode past him, and on out of the room.

Shaw and I returned to our hotel. I retired to my room for a rest. Later that evening we took a stroll to and fro over the Charles Bridge, sometimes stopping and gazing at the river flowing on past. We were leaving for Bratislava the next morning.

Eventually Shaw turned to me and asked, "But who won?"

"It was a draw."

❦

In the morning, there was a package waiting for me at reception. It was from Michaelis. I opened it as I waited for my breakfast eggs to arrive. The parcel contained a turn of the century Baedeker, battered and much-worn. Slipped inside the book was a postcard of the Sternbergstadt town museum. On the back Michaelis had written: *I gave the cricket bats to the museum. They were still there on the day I last left Sternbergstadt—I saw them for myself. They had never been labelled: perhaps a final mystery?*

As I poured my coffee, and spread jam on my roll, I thought about England and Sternbergstadt, of Michaelis, Bradley and Mitchell, the Great War, and the changes it had brought: things once unchangeable and certain transformed into the unknown and frightening. And all those millions of lives altered forever, and those lost. And now the little enigma of a trio of unknown objects in a small museum in an ancient provincial town, symbolising—what?

I had been considering suggesting to the Board of Directors that the company make some plans to expand into South-East Europe and the Balkans. There are boundaries that may be negotiated and crossed over, the web forever circling around the unwanted question.

The Rise and Fall of the SSS

Silently, swiftly, the posters had gone up overnight on walls and fences all over Sternbergstadt. Men trudging to work, women on their way to market, and children dawdling on their way to school all saw the multicoloured sheets splashed over their town. Most took no notice: new posters were always appearing, before being pasted over, defaced, or simply removed. But a small number of citizens stopped and looked; and of them a few took note of the text printed beneath the enigmatic emblem prominent on each poster.

As the bells of the Lutheran church finished chiming six, Florian Capraru stopped outside the gate to the steps leading up to the cemetery on Star Hill. Several posters had been hurriedly pasted on the brickwork; one of them was already beginning to peel away from the wall. Capraru looked around. Unobserved, he quickly smoothed the poster back into place. Then he stood back and considered the symbol on it. He peered at the device as if he had never seen it before in his life. But this was purely for the benefit of anyone walking past at that early hour. Florian Capraru had in fact been responsible for the design and layout of the posters. And along with the other founder members, he had been out in the streets of Steaua de Munte throughout the darkest hours of the night, evading policemen and watchmen, helping to festoon the town and its suburbs: informing everyone who cared to take any notice of the fact that the SSS had been born.

"Tell me, what is this thing, this SSS?"

Capraru recognised the voice. He forced himself not to burst out laughing. There were more people on the streets now. "Dr. Henningsdorf, we have done well, I think. All Steaua de Munte will know about the SSS by noon."

"Yes indeed! Well done, Florian. And goodbye for now." Henningsdorf hurried away.

Capraru continued to gaze at the poster. He was proud of it. At the top were the three letters SSS (in a Moderne style) enclosed within two horizontal lines which met in the circumference of a circle that surrounded them. In turn the circle was embedded inside a shape which some had thought looked like a distorted and badly printed arrow. This pointed up to the right at an angle of about forty-five degrees, intended to give the impression of movement and flight. In fact Capraru had gained his inspiration from *Frau im Mond*, which had played at the Cinema Ardeal in 1929. He had watched the film several times, and pored over the designs, film stills and all other publicity material that he had been able to lay his hands on.

The distorted arrow was in truth a stylised space rocket; and SSS stood for the Sternbergstadt Spaceflight Society. The Society's emblem occupied the upper two-thirds or so of the poster; under that was printed: Public meeting: Union Hall, Vaselor Street: 25 June 1930 at 1900. Main speaker: Prof. Dr. Hermann Oberth. *Per ardua ad astra!*

Professor Karl Henningsdorf—the self-appointed Chairman of the SSS—had deliberately decided to use the initials of the English version of the full name, in order to avoid the necessity of having to print it in triplicate, in Romanian, German, and Magyar. He had summed up his reasoning when he had declared: "It doesn't matter what people actually call it, just as long as they know that we are the SSS and what we stand for." (Once, after a fourth glass of schnapps, Henningsdorf had been heard to state that, in his view, it was a matter of great convenience that the Romanian, German, and Magyar names for the town all began with the letter S; but it was such a great pity that he could only ever learn to pronounce the name of his birthplace in no more than two out of the three languages.)

Capraru remembered that Nicolae Zaituc had said to Henningsdorf, "But you haven't even yet invited Dr. Oberth! How do you know he will be able to come?"

"No, of course I haven't invited him," the Chairman replied irritably. "But his name will help to guarantee a larger audience. Even though he's originally from Hermannstadt—all right, all right, Sibiu—and I'm sure would support the aims of the SSS, he's not going to travel all the way from Berlin or wherever just to talk to us. Not yet, anyway. When our first rocket is finally ready, when we've done all the tests—then we'll invite him, and then he'll want to come. For our first meeting, I will be the main speaker. They know me here."

Exactly, Capraru had thought to himself.

꙯

Doctor Karl Henningsdorf, the main founder, Chairman, and general leading light of the SSS, was Professor of Mechanical Physics and Astronomy at the Technical and Scientific Institute. His doctorate, from the University of Vienna, was genuine; but no-one, least of all his current employers, were sure where Henningsdorf's professorship had come from, who had endowed his Chair, or even precisely what subject it was actually in. But the title had been a part of Henningsdorf's name for as long as anyone could remember. It fitted him like the dusty black top hat he inevitably wore, even for lectures; and, as it was rumoured, for his bath and in his bed. However, it was generally acknowledged beyond any doubt that Dr. Karl Henningsdorf loved his subject, and knew it well. His students testified to that. Nevertheless, the overwhelming majority of the inhabitants of Steaua de Munte at best considered him to be a harmless eccentric; and at worst, mad and dangerous.

As a rule Henningsdorf's students gained excellent marks and proceeded to the better universities. In class their teacher and mentor entertained them, and they cheerfully left his lectures often without even realising that they had understood him and gained knowledge in the process. Of course, like all academics that make their living by giving lectures, Henningsdorf could on occasion digress from his planned theme. The previous year, when he was in the middle of a lecture on the composition of the upper atmosphere, he revealed that he had written a novel during his holiday the previous summer. It was called *Out of the Atmosphere*, and dealt with the firing of a large missile at the Moon, carrying a man and a dog as passengers, and their experiences once they had arrived there. The novel had not so far been published in Romania, Henningsdorf had said, but it was in the process of being translated into English for a magazine of scientific fiction in the United States edited and published by Hugo Gernsback. "But it will not always remain fiction," he had told his students. "The details are technically accurate. One day such a voyage will happen. And the dog is neither here nor there." When *Frau im Mond* was released, some of Henningsdorf's students reminded him of what he had said. Henningsdorf swept off his top hat and bowed. "You see, gentlemen, it is only a matter of time."

Karl Henningsdorf lived in two large rooms that he rented at the Seven Stars House. Every morning over his breakfast coffee and rolls, with jam, cheese, and gherkins, Henningsdorf glanced at a newspaper, and then settled down to skim through the pile of scientific journals, academic papers, magazines, and letters that invariably awaited him. He always looked forward to the latest issue of *Amazing Stories*, especially sent over from the United States, and would gaze for a long time at the gaudy cover painting by his favourite artist, Frank R. Paul, before riffling through the pages and staring in turn at the interior illustrations, many of which were also by Paul. Then Henningsdorf would glance through the rest of his mail.

One morning there were letters from Hermann Oberth, Robert H. Goddard, and Konstantin Tsiolkovsky. Enclosed with Oberth's letter was a brochure proclaiming the continuing activities of the *Verein für Raumschiffahrt*—the Society for Space Travel—and inviting Henningsdorf to join. He thought that what had been inaugurated in Breslau could also be taken up in Sternbergstadt. What about a Romanian version of the Society for Space Travel? It could be part of a great international and cosmopolitan scientific undertaking; just the sort of thing that was needed in these politically difficult times. Henningsdorf gulped down the rest of his coffee, pushed his magazines and letters into his briefcase, and strode out of the hotel.

❧

Union Hall could easily hold two hundred people, and that number of chairs had been put out in serried ranks in front of the stage. At the front of the stage was a lectern with a chair directly behind it; and off to one side and further to the rear were a table and three more chairs. Florian

Capraru placed three glasses of water on the desk and one on the lectern. He was hot and tired: along with another of Dr. Henningsdorf's students—also a founder member of the new SSS—he had spent the afternoon helping the hall caretaker dragging piles of chairs out from their storeroom and arranging them. Capraru and his friend Zaituc were hefty and strong young men; Henningsdorf had chosen them not only for their intelligence and interest in the SSS, but also for their size and strength. The Chairman had explained that it was not only building the SSS rocket that would require physical as well as mental labour—being able and willing to keep order at public meetings and other events, if the need arose, was also desirable. Henningsdorf had decreed that their membership of the SSS would be "free, gratis, and for nothing, as the Americans say" as a token of his appreciation for their help in the potentially two very different spheres of the Society's activities.

At half-past six Henningsdorf bustled into the hall. He looked approvingly at the empty rows of chairs and at the large SSS emblem that Capraru had just finished attaching to the back wall behind the table.

"Well, well, gentlemen!" Henningsdorf beamed. "All is ready, and in good time too, I see! I am sure they will be arriving at any moment now."

He nodded at Capraru and Zaituc. Then he turned to Capraru. "After the meeting I want to discuss the SSS magazine with you—"

"What magazine?"

"Haven't I mentioned it? I think the SSS should produce a publication of its own. It need not be anything too elaborate to begin with. I have written a paper, and the Breslau group and the Russians will correspond with us. It could serialise my novel. And we need a cover design, and a suitable name. I had thought about *The Transylvania Star in Space*. What do you think?"

Capraru was speechless for a few seconds. "We still have to get this meeting out of the way first, Professor," he said. "And they're not exactly breaking the doors down to get in, are they?"

"We've got half an hour to go yet. No-one can say they don't know about the meeting."

At seven o'clock Henningsdorf climbed up the wooden steps to the stage. Nicolae Zaituc leaned over and nudged Capraru. "The old boy doesn't look downhearted at all. He should be mounting those steps like he was going to the scaffold!"

Capraru shook his head. "He won't give up easily—not him." He looked out over the ranks of chairs sweeping away from the stage to the back of the hall. They were all nearly empty, apart from the front row, where a few seats were occupied. Other occupied seats were dotted around the space of the hall like rocks jutting up from a calm sea. The caretaker lounged at the back, and there was a uniformed policeman standing by the entrance. Glancing around the hall, Capraru estimated that the audience was about fifteen in total.

Henningsdorf strode to the lectern. He pushed his hat back slightly and pulled a sheet of paper from his pocket. He unfolded it and laid it on the lectern. He gazed out over the hall, moving his head from side to side as if he were taking in a great multitude filling all the seats. "My friends! You are privileged! I welcome you to the inaugural meeting of the SSS—the Sternbergstadt Spaceflight Society! The future begins today, here and now!" He drank some water. "My dear friends, the last century saw unparalleled progress. Over the decades humanity has conquered land and sea. Railways and roads hold the world in their embrace, and there is no mighty mountain or abyssal gorge that cannot now be bypassed by tunnel or bridge. Tremendous liners and commercial vessels cross and re-cross the oceans and seas, their voyages carrying people and cargo to distant places like the life-blood of a healthy body. Submarines glide through the sunless depths." Henningsdorf paused, and took a sip of water. "My friends, this great twentieth century has witnessed the opening of humanity's conquest of the air. From the smallest beginnings, aircraft and airships are now able to circle the world, linking the greatest empires and the smallest states!" He paused again and gazed out over his audience. If he was dismayed by the small size of it, he showed no outward sign. Then he continued his address, his voice low and gradually rising in volume. "That conquest of the air is still in its infancy. The best is still to come. But there is yet another conquest to be undertaken, and which awaits us here and now. My dear friends, I refer to—the conquest of space!"

Capraru and Zaituc started to applaud. The students in the front row broke into applause as well; most of the other listeners did not move their hands, but continued to sit still, stony-faced and silent. Henningsdorf gestured for silence.

"My friends, I have said that the conquest of space awaits us. And so it does. But it has already begun—make no mistake about that, ladies and gentlemen. In the United States, in Russia, in Germany—yes, in Germany, spearheaded by that native son of our own glorious Transylvania, Dr. Hermann Oberth—"

Someone sitting towards the back of the hall got up and shouted: "Where's Oberth? We want Oberth! Not you—Oberth!"

Henningsdorf gave his heckler a broad smile. "My dear sir, he is not able to be with us tonight—"

"What! Did his rocket blow up or something? We want Oberth!"

"I have a telegram," Henningsdorf shouted. He tugged a piece of paper from his waistcoat pocket and waved it in the air. "Here. Dr. Oberth regrets that his absence is inevitable, due to unavoidable circumstances. But he sends the SSS—he sends *us*—his most cordial greetings and very best wishes. He will attend the first launching of our first rocket into the upper air, the threshold of space!"

The students started clapping again. Zaituc whispered to Capraru, "He made that telegram up, didn't he?"

"My friends, my friends! Yes! Our own rocket! I hereby announce to you that we here, today, in our fine city, have banded together to play our part in the development of the world; of humanity's magnificent progress from earth-bound dreamer to possessor of the planets and stars!"

Henningsdorf gulped down the rest of his water, wiped his forehead, and sat down heavily on the chair behind the lectern. Several people started to applaud; there was a small amount of cheering. The heckler stalked out of the hall. The policeman was joined by a man in civilian clothes. In the aisle, Henningsdorf shook the hands of the students who had remained behind.

Capraru moved the lectern away as the hall caretaker started pointedly slamming doors. "Do you know who that heckler was?" Zaituc asked.

"I can tell you're not from here," Capraru laughed. "That's Stancu. I don't know his first name. He's the town pest. Drunk most of the time, as well, I reckon. Don't you have anyone like that in Brașov?"

"Plenty!"

"Grab the banner," Capraru said. "Then let's go and keep the Professor company, shall we? I don't like the look of those policemen. It's *per ardua* all right!"

45

❦

At six o'clock the next morning Florian Capraru was again standing next to the gate at the bottom of the Star Hill steps. The SSS posters had been torn from the wall, and there were now no more to be seen over the entire town. He heard the footsteps approaching.

"Good morning, Florian," Henningsdorf said. "Well, perhaps the meeting did not go quite as well as I had expected. I am still somewhat tired: I am always in my bed by eleven o'clock. And here I was, removing posters in the New Town until nearly dawn. I must say, you did put them up well, Florian."

Capraru yawned. He had not actually been to bed. "Nicolae and the others have done their best, too."

"Yes, yes, I'm sure. I will make certain I thank them. And thank you again, Florian." He hesitated. "Would you care to join me for breakfast?"

Henningsdorf was silent throughout the meal. The two men were drinking the last of their coffee when the Professor suddenly said: "You do believe in what I want to do, and the SSS, don't you? Really?"

"Well . . . "

"I knew it!"

"No, no, please listen. I do support you. I'm just not sure announcing the SSS like this was such a good idea . . . But that's done now, isn't it? We'll work with that. Now, have you actually contacted Dr. Oberth yet?"

"I will, when we have all in place for our first launch. Now, Florian, I have one more favour to ask. Would you kindly accompany me to the Town Hall? As you know, I have to be there at nine o'clock. We will have time to shave and change clothes."

At a quarter to nine Capraru and Henningsdorf reached the end of the High Street and began climbing the steps that led up to the top of Castle Hill, and to the old Castle itself, part of which had served as the Town Hall for at least two hundred years. They plodded up the wide stone steps, which curled around the slope of the hill and clung to it like a vine wrapping itself around a pillar. They wandered around the outer courtyard until the town's clocks started to strike nine; then they headed straight for the Mayor's office.

The Mayor was waiting for them. "Good morning, gentlemen. Inspector Gilca will be joining us in just a moment. I have his full report, however. Tell me, Professor Henningsdorf, this Space Travel Club—"

"It's the Sternbergstadt Spaceflight Society."

"Yes, of course. It was, ah, very well advertised. As you will remember, the inspector was deeply concerned; and, therefore, now am I. Professor Henningsdorf, I am not a young man, but I am somewhat younger than you, and I did fight with our army in Hungary against Béla Kun in 1919. Naturally I believe that conflict and its result were just; but I would not wish the experience on my worst enemy."

Henningsdorf looked blank. He turned to Capraru. Then Inspector Gilca entered the office.

"Please sit down, gentlemen," the Mayor said. "Inspector, I was trying to explain some of my misgivings to the Professor and his young friend here. I said that I had experienced warfare, and if that taught me anything, it was that projectiles are dangerous and to be avoided. Yes, most definitely. The loss of life was gigantic. In the war, I mean."

Inspector Gilca spoke slowly, as if to a child. "Professor, during the war I was with the King—God rest him—in Iaşi. I saw at first-hand what such weapons can do. What the Mayor is trying to say, and what I say also, based on what you told me last night, is that the police, the Town Council, the county authorities, and—if I should bring

47

this to their attention, the authorities in Bucharest—have very considerable misgivings about what you want to do. Rockets! Projectiles! Where would you fire these from? Where would they go?"

Capraru would have kicked Henningsdorf on the shin, but the Inspector had placed himself between them.

"Where from? Where to? What for?" said Henningsdorf, as if he had to address a class of backward students. His previous nervousness had evaporated. "What makes you think that I know nothing about what you speak of? Why, it is precisely to assist humanity's progress towards peace and the brotherhood of science that I founded the Sternbergstadt Spaceflight Society. Frontiers down here are becoming meaningless. The greater frontier beckons! Item one: that is why I wish to build a rocket to penetrate the outer reaches of this planet's atmosphere. Item two: I want to go on to build rockets that will carry men into space: to the Moon, to Mars and beyond. Item three: I want to make this city world-famous as the departure point for these great voyages of exploration and discovery. And four: to begin with, we will use Star Hill. It's high up and empty. There's no-one there but dead people. And moreover, they're all dead Germans, my ancestors. They built and ran this city when they were alive, but that was in the past. And now, they will contribute to its future even though they are dead! They still serve their country! What do you think of that, gentlemen?"

Capraru put his head into his hands, closed his eyes and sighed deeply.

❧

"The Professor was so lucky that all he got was a good telling-off," Capraru explained to Zaituc. "The Mayor and that police inspector as much as threatened that they would go to Bucharest and get the powers that be to take action against him and the SSS."

"Which means us as well," Zaituc said. "Florian, I have my future career to think about. So do you. Maybe Henningsdorf went too far this time."

"Too far? You should have seen him. He hasn't started yet. All right, he agreed not to do anything on Star Hill, or anywhere else, but he didn't agree not to do anything outside of the town boundary. He still wants to build and launch a rocket, and his dream of putting this town on the map is as strong as ever. You know the Professor."

Henningsdorf came back into the sitting room. He held a cardboard tube in his hand. Sitting down opposite his students, he extracted a rolled-up map from the tube, and spread it flat on the table between them. He placed a cup or glass at each corner of the map. The built-up area of Sternbergstadt—the Old Town within the walls, the New Town, the modern suburbs and industrial areas—was a black blot in the centre of the map, caught in a web of roads and lanes radiating out from it. The river meandered across the paper landscape, and the railway sliced across it, touching the edge of the New Town before vanishing again into the country off the edge of the map.

"Let me follow the road here," Henningsdorf said, pointing at where Bridge Street crossed the river, and moving his finger through the rectilinear streets and squares of the New Town. "See, past the station, and out into the countryside, beyond the town limits. There's where the boundary is marked. Now I carry on for another two kilometres or so, and—there!" He stabbed his finger at the map.

"What is it? What's there?" Zaituc asked.

"My dear Nicolae, it is the farm of Mr. Petrescu. I know him well. He will rent me—the SSS, rather—a barn and the use of the farmyard. Because of its location the farm is outside the control of the Town Council, and what the police and the county people in Sibiu don't know won't worry them. Are you still with me, gentlemen?"

Capraru and Zaituc looked at each other.

"Excellent, gentlemen! Now, to work!"

⁂

Over the next year, Henningsdorf and his small group of dedicated followers spent much of their time out at Petrescu's farm. The Professor continued to give his lectures and tutorials as usual, but outside of his contracted hours at the Technical and Scientific Institute he was more often to be found poring over plans and diagrams in the barn rather than his rooms in the town. Henningsdorf gave Capraru and Zaituc detailed instructions to take to two skilled metal-workers in towns far beyond the county boundary; he spent evenings checking and testing the metal tubes and oddly-shaped containers that came back. Often they were returned for modifications. On one occasion, Henningsdorf smashed an entire consignment of valves with a hammer, shouting for them to be melted down and made all over again.

The SSS discovered only one real disadvantage with working in secret in Petrescu's barn. And that wasn't the time spent travelling to and from Sternbergstadt, usually in Zaituc's decrepit car, or the necessity of having to work by the flickering light of oil lamps, or the regular invasion by one of Petrescu's cows, who always seemed to be able to get into the barn, despite all measures taken to keep the doors securely closed. And that disadvantage was that Petrescu's chief drinking partner was Ion Stancu. Petrescu kept his word to Henningsdorf about maintaining absolute secrecy concerning what he had rented out his barn for. But when Stancu visited the farm, Petrescu couldn't guarantee to stop his friend from wandering around where he shouldn't be and where he certainly wasn't wanted.

Capraru encountered Stancu first. Henningsdorf and Zaituc had driven back to the Technical Institute, leaving Capraru to tidy up, lock everything away and secure the barn, before cycling home. He had just closed the doors and put the padlock on them when he heard footsteps behind him. He turned round.

"Hey rocket man, what's going on? What're you doing? What've you got in there? Hey?" He swayed slightly as he stood there. "And where's Oberth?"

"What do you want, Stancu?" Capraru said. "No, don't answer that. Just go away. Go home."

"Not until I know what you and the old professor rocket man are up to. I was at that meeting where Oberth wasn't, and I know the police had words with you afterwards. You got into trouble, and you're up to no good now. I know it. I'll go to the Town Hall right now—"

Capraru thought quickly. "All right, Stancu, wait a moment. You can have a look, just one. But there's nothing to see." Capraru unlocked the barn doors again and opened them. "There."

Stancu staggered forwards and leaned into the barn, gripping the side of the door. "There're just piles of rubbish. Pipes and old kettles." He looked around in the gloom. "What're those?" He pointed at several large metal drums of liquid that had been delivered the previous day, to be used to make up the mixture for fuel. "What's in them?"

"It's what we use for the fuel. It's ethanol."

Stancu nodded deliberately, as if he had just been let into a great secret. "Etho-whatever, hey?" He sniffed. "Tell you what, it smells like what I get from Müller's stall in the market, when I'm a bit short of a few lei." He licked his lips. "It does the job when I need it though."

Capraru slammed the doors shut and locked them again. He gave Stancu a worn and creased banknote. "Get yourself some plum brandy. And you'd better forget I let you see inside here. If you don't, you might be the one having to visit the police. I know what Müller also keeps in that box under his stall for his even more special customers."

Eventually a rocket engine was completed to Henningsdorf's satisfaction. On paper everything was as it should be. It remained to be seen if that would be the case in reality. The engine was securely bolted and welded to an old anvil, which had been partly buried in the hard earth floor of the barn. Reinforced pipes led to where small feeder tanks of ethanol and liquid oxygen were to be positioned. Capraru filled the ethanol tank and checked that its valve was functioning correctly. Zaituc lifted the reinforced and insulated cylinder of liquid oxygen that Henningsdorf had ordered from Bucharest out of his car and gingerly fixed it into place.

"Everything connected?" Henningsdorf said. "Valves ready?"

Both men answered, before walking quickly to the other end of the barn, where the Professor waited.

"For space and country!" Henningsdorf shouted, as he threw the switches to open the valves. A moment later he pressed a button to produce the igniting spark. The engine roared into life: a sharp pale blue jet of flame shot out several metres and the barn started to shake. Some glass containers on the table vibrated and seemed in danger of sliding over the edge, on to the floor. But the engine stayed firmly attached to the anvil, and after about ten seconds the fuel ran out and the flame died away as suddenly as it had exploded into life. The new silence in the barn was deafening. Henningsdorf threw the switches that closed the valves.

"It's still in one piece. It works! Oberth, Goddard, Tsiolkovsky, here we come!" Henningsdorf leaped up and performed a little dance, jumping up and down, raising and lowering his top hat. "Well done! Sternbergstadt in space!" He pumped Capraru's and Zaituc's hands so vigorously that they thought he would pull them off. He danced around the barn. "I've had a terrific idea. I'll offer young Prince Mihai a little model rocket for his birthday! He'll have the time now."

That evening Henningsdorf took Capraru and Zaituc out to dinner at the Restaurant de Paris. The three men drank toasts to the SSS, and made their final plans as the meal progressed.

"Now you can invite Dr. Oberth," Capraru said.

"Yes! And I'll even invite that drunken troublemaker Stancu—that'll show you how pleased I am," Henningsdorf replied. "The Mayor and Gilca can also have the pleasure of his company for once."

❧

Two large SSS banners had been placed on the front of Petrescu's barn, one on each door.

"Where's the Professor?" asked Capraru.

"He's still in the barn, checking the gyroscopes. He said he'd call us when he needs our help with the rocket. He's been in there all night, guarding everything."

Capraru consulted his watch. The dignitaries should be here any moment now. He did actually invite Dr. Oberth this time, didn't he?"

"Yes, and Stancu. I think Stancu stayed the night in the house with Petrescu. Yesterday evening he said they were going to have a few drinks as a sort of advance celebration and toast."

"Huh. I don't think Stancu knows the meaning of 'few'. And you still think he's never told anyone about all this, Nicolae?"

"Well, he swore he hadn't, and you know Petrescu would tell the Professor if he thought that the secret was out."

Capraru nodded. "Well, the Mayor and Gilca will be in for a pleasant surprise, then. The reporters should be here by now. I sent the details to all the big newspapers in Transylvania, as well as the main ones in Bucharest, Ploieşti, Constanţa, and Iaşi. And I contacted the other rocket societies." The sound of grinding gears made the men turn to face the road. Three cars toiled slowly along the rutted track towards the barn and farmyard. Two uniformed policemen jumped out of the front of the first car, and opened the rear doors for their passengers. Inspector Gilca and the Mayor climbed out and strode over to where Capraru and Zaituc were standing. More policemen got out of the second car; the third car contained Emil Harnack, editor of the *Sternbergstadt Daily Times*, and another man equipped with a film camera, which he immediately began to set up.

"As it's old Henningsdorf, I thought I'd come out here myself," Harnack laughed. "And get it all on film as well. So what's new?" He shook hands with Capraru and Zaituc, then Gilca and the Mayor.

"Where's Henningsdorf?" asked Inspector Gilca. "I thought we had an agreement. No experiments, no rockets, missiles, bombs—"

One of the barn doors opened part of the way and Henningsdorf walked out of the dimness and into the bright daylight.

"Within the town limits, gentlemen. This building is a long way beyond them. I and my colleagues are here with the owner's consent. We have done nothing whatsoever wrong. When the King and Prime Minister themselves thank us for putting Romania at the forefront of the exploration of the universe, then you'll laugh on the other side of your faces." He glared at the policemen and the Mayor. "I think it would be best if you stand over there, by the house. Florian, Nicolae: the doors, please."

The young men opened the doors of the barn slowly and deliberately. The lamp-lit gloom within vanished, and revealed the rocket, standing within its supporting framework of scaffolding, which in turn rested on a low, flat, four-wheeled carrying vehicle. The vertical supports were slotted firmly into the base of the carrier, the wooden floor of which was covered over with sheets of iron. One man stood on either side of the rocket. At a signal from Henningsdorf, they each grasped a welded handle, and slowly propelled the rocket out into the full light of day. Gilca and the Mayor stood dumbfounded. Henningsdorf returned to the barn and wheeled out a device looking like a small lectern with switches and buttons on the sloping face. Wires trailed on the ground behind him; he picked up the loose ends and slotted them into sockets on the side of the rocket platform, tightening the screws to hold them in place.

"There. That's done. I've connected up the tanks," Henningsdorf said. "I sat in my chair by the rocket all night, after I'd pumped in the ethanol. The rats or whatever the noise was kept me awake, but I'm not at all tired." He looked around the farmyard. "Where's everyone else?"

The front door of the farmhouse opened behind them. "Where's everyone else, you old fool? Where's Oberth? We want Oberth! Oberth! Oberth! Hey!"

Zaituc rushed over to where Stancu was staggering out of the house. He grasped Stancu's shoulders and pushed him down, making him sit on top of an upturned barrel. "Just sit there and shut up."

Capraru ran over to Professor Henningsdorf. "It's all right. Old Stancu's been drinking all night, that's all. He's harmless. Everything is ready."

Inspector Gilca said, "We're here now, so we'll see this through. But I'm warning you, Professor. If anything goes wrong . . . I've got my men here. You'll be finished. And your young friends, too."

"Florian, why isn't Oberth here?" Henningsdorf asked plaintively.

"He must be delayed. But we can't wait any more. The weather's fine, there's hardly any breeze. The rocket is standing free. We have to launch now."

Stancu belched loudly, and tried to stand up. Petrescu came out of the house and made him sit back down again. The assembled experimenters and spectators caught a whiff of Stancu's breath and winced.

"Smells like that gut-rot old Müller sells in the market," one of the policemen whispered to his colleague.

Stancu was muttering incoherently to Petrescu, who tried to listen to him and understand what he was telling him, yet not be overpowered by the fumes of his breath. Suddenly Petrescu broke away and ran over to Henningsdorf.

"Karl, I think you should hear this—"

"No, no, not now, Theodor!" Henningsdorf threw the switches, and a moment later, pressed a button. "Valves— open! Spark—now!"

For a second nothing happened. Then a blue flame roared from the base of the rocket, and it strained upwards in the midst of its supports. It rose a few centimetres, before the flame abruptly cut out. The rocket dropped back onto its platform with a dull clang. Metal buckled, and the rocket stood tilted at a slight angle, held up by the scaffolding.

Henningsdorf closed the switches, staring at the rocket as if he were in a trance. He pushed his top hat back on his head. The cameraman was filming for all he was worth; Capraru and Zaituc stared open-mouthed at the motionless rocket. Gilca, the policemen, and the Mayor walked back to their cars. "I'd like to see you at my office at nine o'clock tomorrow, Professor," the Mayor called out. "*If* you please."

Henningsdorf continued to stand rooted to the spot. After a few minutes he started to smile, as if he had remembered a joke. The newspapermen drove away.

"Florian, Nicolae, we must continue. After I've been to the Town Hall—" Then he realised Petrescu was still standing next to him, trying to attract his attention. "Yes, Theodor? You wanted to say something?" he asked gently.

"You won't like this," Petrescu said.

"What could I not like now? Please tell me, Theodor, old friend."

"I can tell you why your rocket didn't move. You know, that wasn't rats you heard out in the barn. I haven't got rats in there. You drove them all out, with that thing and all the noise and flames. Last night Stancu was drinking all the time and I was watching him, like I said I would. But he kept on having to go outside as you must, for, you know, and well—you can guess. Stancu and that rocket stuff are like Carol and Lupescu. You can't separate them. I'm sorry, Karl."

Henningsdorf turned and gazed at Petrescu for a long minute. "That's quite all right, Theodor. I know how it is." Then he spoke to Capraru. "Florian, would you and Nicolae please put everything back in the barn? Then please find this loose plank and repair it? And then lock the doors?

Thank you, gentlemen. I need to have a little talk with Mr. Stancu. I hope I will see you back at the Institute."

Henningsdorf and Petrescu pulled Stancu up from where he was slumped on the barrel, and dragged him into the house. The door slammed shut behind them.

"Lucky Oberth didn't show up," Zaituc said. "If he had done I think he might've witnessed a man being launched into the upper atmosphere! At least there's nothing else that can go wrong." The two men wheeled the rocket back into the barn. They took down the SSS banners from the doors.

Capraru and Zaituc had just finished locking up the barn when a car turned into the yard and stopped in front of them.

The Reluctant Visionary

Now

The turn of the new century was a time of great opportunity. I was newly qualified as an architect, living in Bucharest, and the work never stopped coming in to the office. Since the Revolution in 1989 Romania had been slowly remaking its links with Central and Western Europe; putting back the connections that had been severely reduced since the 1940s. The infrastructure of large areas of the country's cities had been neglected for forty years; in Bucharest the Communist government had swept away a vast area of the old city to make way for its so-called Palace of the People and the enormous boulevards and squares that went with it. All over Romania there was a gigantic backlog of repairs and improvements to be done, with older buildings needing to be restored or even saved from destruction. In addition, clients were looking towards Romania joining the European Union, and new buildings and infrastructure projects were commissioned by the score. It was a good time to be a young architect—and especially a successful one, as I was.

No-one should think that all I wanted to do was to build glass-walled skyscrapers in Bucharest city centre, or to spend time making sure the Communists' system-built housing blocks—enormous developments spreading out all over the outskirts of the city—were made habitable for the twentieth century, let alone the twenty-first. Not at all.

In reality my main interest was in helping clients to restore surviving buildings from the city's past and make them usable again. Working in conjunction with colleagues from within the firm and contacts from outside it—often local politicians—I also helped clients to secure possession of buildings that could then be saved from demolition or further decay, and made fit for purpose again. Needless to say, this was done to the benefit of all concerned.

Bucharest boasts a singular concentration of modernist architecture from the 1920s and '30s. In the nineteenth and early twentieth century the city had already built wide boulevards and begun to line them with elaborate buildings, which led to it gaining the nickname "Paris of the East". And in the decade before the Second World War, there had been a concerted effort of give Bucharest the most modern appearance then possible, whether for commercial, cultural, public, or private use. Thus several of the boulevards in the city centre came to feature great white apartment blocks like moored ocean liners, with their rows of balconies and windows, stairwells with circular windows like portholes, sleek curves, and flat roofs. Hotels were rebuilt with the best facilities for their day. Office blocks and towers were built in the same style, bringing touches of Manhattan and Chicago to Romania. And cinemas were built—those dream-houses of hope and escape where people could sit in comfort and shiny splendour and be transported into new and different worlds, with dreams of the future and idealised pasts. And I was involved in the purchase and refurbishment of many such buildings, which again graced the boulevards with the original modernist splendour that they had been given before the decades of neglect and deterioration set in.

In many cases it had been possible to locate the original plans and blueprints. I spent my waking hours poring over them, comparing present plans of buildings with their past ones. I also browsed through innumerable bookshops and antique shops, buying up old postcards and photographs that showed the buildings in their original states: gleaming white blocks rising up out of the mass of older and lower buildings, a concrete example, in more ways than one, of the bright and clean future transforming the grimy and cramped past. I started to buy artefacts and furniture from the 1920s and '30s, the sort of items that would have been found inside a newly-completed apartment of the era. Crockery and cutlery, pictures, chairs, wardrobes; even a contemporary radio and phonograph, complete with albums of symphonies, concerti, and jazz music, all on the solid and heavy discs standard at the time. Sometimes I would place some of my expanding collection in the newly-refurbished flats we planned to sell; and occasionally I sold-on items to the purchaser—at, of course, a healthy profit, which I then put into buying more such items whenever and wherever I found them. For my intention was, one day, to buy and furnish such an apartment for myself. I would sit on a terrace high above a boulevard, and relax with my dreams of the cosmopolitan modernist future that had come to such a shattering end in war.

For as long as I could remember, I always carried with me, like a rucksack sitting squarely between my shoulders, nostalgia for the future. And it was a modernist future, involving the architecture and décor I had become so fascinated with. I was born in the Transylvanian town of Steaua de Munte, also known as Sternbergstadt. Although it is an ancient walled town, there is also the baroque New Town, some late nineteenth century boulevards built in imitation of those in Bucharest, and several large modernist apartment blocks built along a broad avenue linking one of the older parts of town with some newer and fast-growing residential suburbs and industrial areas. That entire district, laid-out and developed between 1935 and 1940, resembles a miniature version of Asmara, the worn and dusty modernist jewel that is the capital of Eritrea. But the finest modernist building in Steaua de Munte is a cinema. Originally built as the Kino Mitteleuropa, and long since renamed the Cinema Cosmopolitain, it was built in direct imitation of the Cinema Scala on Magheru Boulevard in Bucharest, except on a reduced scale. The "Cosmo" (as we called it) occupied an entire block on Union Avenue. Like its counterpart in the capital, the exterior consisted of a cliff-like block of apartments, with shops on the ground floor. One end of the block curved round like the stern of a great ocean-going vessel. Next to it was the cinema entrance itself, with a taller square block above. Then there was another block of shops and flats, set back from the frontage of the other blocks, and slightly lower. By the time I knew it, the entire structure presented a somewhat run-down and seedy appearance. The long rows of low windows and railed balconies were grimy and dull, and the white stucco had either flaked away or had become grubby and stained by smoke and dirty rain. The stone and marble mouldings were also dirtied by years of pollution and neglect. But all this made the building somehow more romantic, more of a gateway to the dream worlds that my friends and I had experienced in films—even the films the regime had allowed us to see.

And now I had heard that the entire building was empty and up for sale, with the option of being torn down for total redevelopment. I made a brief visit to my home town and looked around. I called in favours and asked questions. Back in Bucharest I discussed the matter with colleagues and the firm's accountants. I checked my own financial situation. I was living in a grim but cheap apartment on the periphery of the city, and now the years of saving paid off. I sold a few choice items of ceramic and glass; and a few sought-after books that I'd bought for a song. Eventually a small consortium put together from members of my firm of architects became the owners of the Cinema Cosmopolitain complex—with me as the majority shareholder.

I moved back to Steaua de Munte to superintend the restoration and refurbishment. My parents were pleased to see me, and I was able to live with them at almost no cost. I used my connections with the town to the full. I performed the role of a native son returning, successful, bringing work and with the promise of more. I visited people, made presentations, and negotiated, helping all the bureaucratic processes along in a variety of ways. I made it clear that the consortium intended to ensure that only the best shops were allowed to rent premises on the ground floor, and that we would restore and reopen the cinema itself, although I decided to keep the Cinema Cosmopolitain name. We wished to attract foreign tourists as well as play a part in regenerating the local commercial and arts infrastructures for the inhabitants of Steaua de Munte. In the long-term I planned to buy out the consortium and become sole owner of the property; and in preparation for that I continued to live frugally, replenishing my financial resources and trying to make sure that the investment would pay back the highest possible return. I bought an option on a large top-floor apartment, which I created by merging two smaller ones. My rooms would have long, low windows stretching from wall to wall; the balcony—as good as a small terrace—would occupy the sweeping curve at one end of the building. I planned on restoring the original modernist décor where possible, and furnishing the apartment with my collection of artefacts, pictures, maps, and books from the period.

As I have said, since childhood I have experienced a profound longing, nostalgia for the future. In German there is the evocative word *Sehnsucht* for that sort of emotion: a yearning, almost a craving, for something. But in my case it was not the past, or something lost, but a future, symbolised for me by the clean curves, unbroken lines and suppressed power of modernist architecture, with its ranks of large windows, balconies and roof-gardens, careful use of metal and stone, sculpture and decoration, tall slim towers rising in white splendour above the mundane architecture of most ordinary buildings; soaring above them as if pointing up into a transmuted future which had left behind the chaos, dirt, disorder, and irrationalities of the world I actually had to live in.

The restoration and refurbishment proceeded as planned. Our agents sold leases to the owners of good shops, and we were careful in our choice of tenants for the apartments. The Cinema Cosmopolitain was reconstructed to its original design in full—but with the latest screening facilities, of course—and a suitable man was found to manage it. We intended that the restored Cosmo Block (as we had nicknamed the entire complex) would become a major architectural attraction in Steaua de Munte, alongside Castle Hill, Star Square, and the restored Sinaia Boulevard.

When I moved into my apartment I gave a party for the other members of the consortium, the builders, decorators, and others involved, as well as their families. Although I never wanted to feel that I was living in a museum, I have always been careful of my surroundings and their furnishings, so the drinks and food were placed in a vacant apartment next to mine, and I gave tours of my apartment to a few friends at a time, making sure that they were careful about where they put down their plates and glasses. Everyone was genuinely pleased to see what I had done to such a fine building, and the party went very well indeed. Later that night—or early the next morning, rather—as I lay in bed, with the moonlight streaming through the long low windows, I felt that for once in my life I had truly achieved something of lasting value. Now I could start to enjoy it.

I returned to Bucharest a few days later. I started a routine of working in Bucharest during the week, returning to Steaua de Munte late on Friday night and travelling back early on the Monday morning, which gave me the entire two days of the weekend in my home town. When I wasn't involved with the Cosmo Block, and looking for extra things for my apartment, I started to explore Steaua de Munte in ways that I had never done before. I bought maps and guidebooks both old and new; I walked the streets of the Old Town within the walls, the New Town, Parisville and the newer suburbs and quarters built during the twentieth century. I walked through squares and parks and industrial areas, and along both banks of the river. I got to know my own home town in a way that I never had when I lived there as a child and adolescent. I realised that a man has to leave somewhere or something, or to lose it and then regain it, in order to truly appreciate it. I felt that I had regained something with Steaua de Munte.

One Saturday afternoon as I walked back to my apartment after lunch, I noticed that Mihai Lereanu had finally opened his new bookshop, so I decided to go in and have a look around. When Lereanu had signed the lease I told him that I was interested in old maps and guides to Steaua de Munte; he said that he would keep an eye open for me. His shop displayed a bright selection of new novels in one window, and a collection of scarce editions of books by H.G. Wells in the other. I had always loved Wells's novels: I felt that he had shared the same nostalgia for the future that I had. One of my prize possessions I kept in the main bookcase in my apartment was an edition of *The Shape of Things to Come*, bound in a metallic embossed Art Deco cover and including a set of stills from *Things to Come*, the film that was made from it. Some of the photos depicted the machines and cities of Wells's imagined future, all in the Streamlined Moderne of the mid 1930s, but still to me always expressing striving for a clean and trouble-free future.

Lereanu and I shook hands. "What's new?" I said.

"I think you've seen the Wells novels before," he said. "But I have a Baedeker, 1890, superb condition, with maps showing Steaua de Munte—"

"Sternbergstadt, in those days!"

Lereanu grinned. "Yes, of course. The maps show the town just before the first boulevards were built, so they have the street layout where Sinaia Boulevard and Revolution Square are now. And Sternbergstadt itself is fully described, naturally."

"Interesting . . . "

"And I have a box of old postcards. I'm sure they're worth a closer look. Plenty of views of the town, and Bucharest, and all sorts of other places and buildings."

"May I take them home and look at them there?" I asked.

"Yes, that would be fine. I had them ready for you in any case." Lereanu handed me a shoebox. Inside, the book and postcards were carefully wrapped in red tissue paper. I tucked it under my arm as I continued to look along the shelves. I noticed what looked like an old photograph album, wedged in amongst some new acquisitions. It was thick and heavy, and the black leather covers, tooled with an Art Nouveau design, were ingrained with dust. I flicked through the pages. Most were empty, never having been filled; but the first third or so of the album contained plenty of photographs, and at a cursory glance many of them looked to be of Sternbergstadt.

"I'll take a look at this as well, if I may," I said, and left the shop.

Once back in my main room, the one with the curving balcony wall, I put the Baedeker and postcards down on a small table by the door and sat down to look through the photograph album. The photographs seemed to date from the first half of the 1930s. I removed each one carefully; some were inscribed with dates and names on the back. There were several photos of buildings and street scenes in Steaua de Munte, all of places still recognisable. There was a photo of the newly-built Kino Mitteleuropa, and another, presumably taken at the same time, showing the entrance to the cinema with a group of young people standing in front of it. Both seemed to have been taken in bright sunshine: the walls of the cinema gleamed and strong black shadows were cast against it. On the back of the photo was written "Things to come (?) 1936". I picked up a magnifying glass and examined the photo with care. I saw that the film playing at the cinema was the Wells/Korda film. Perhaps these young people were a group of close friends who had been to watch the film together. There were four young men and women: two couples, judging by the way they stood in relation to each other; one of the couples was holding hands, and all were smiling. I thought there was more behind their smiles than just looking at the camera: something of a tense attitude as well. The couple who were not holding hands seemed to be standing in a slightly strained stance, as if they had both suddenly stopped in the middle of a movement and weren't sure of how to resume them when the opportunity came. It looked as if the woman was raising her hand to shield her eyes from the sun, but had stopped when she realised the photograph was about to be taken. Her companion seemed to have been caught in the act of trying to retrieve her arm. Perhaps a lovers' quarrel had been inadvertently captured by the camera.

The question mark on the reverse was perplexing, as if whoever had written the comment hadn't been sure of the film, even though it was clear to see on the posters displayed behind them. Then I noticed that the words did perhaps form a question rather than make a statement. Which of those young men and women had written it, or had someone else? I laid the photograph to one side and continued leafing through the album. There were several other photos of the young man and woman who had perhaps quarrelled; and a few of the woman on her own. I carried on flicking through the unfilled pages at the back, and one of the pages caught on my thumb. It seemed to be thicker than all the others. When I examined it closely, I found that two pages were stuck together, it seemed deliberately. I started to gently ease the pages apart, and before long I pulled out several sheets of paper that must have been hidden away there. They had been cut from a notebook or exercise book, and were closely covered with neat, sharp handwriting in black ink. It was the same handwriting that was on the backs of the photos. It had not faded at all: the pages had surely been hidden away from sight for at least seventy years. They would present no problem to read. I opened a bottle of dark beer, and settled down with them.

Then

Sunday. It was a great film at the Kino Mitteleuropa. We are lucky that the manager is sympathetic to such films as

Things to Come. (Although there must be the commercial considerations as well—no doubt he will be showing only gangster films, musicals, and the vile Nazi *Triumph of the Will* for the next few months!) Adela was in a distracted mood before the film and throughout. She worries me. Maybe we're beginning to drift apart. But the film took my mind off any troubles for a couple of hours. From the solemn opening music, with its cascading chords, all so full of foreboding, to the final scenes with their mounting tension and cosmic ending, I hardly moved. The subtitles weren't as distracting as I'd been expecting, and I'd been able to understand a lot of the dialogue, anyway. As the final sounds died away, I thought that I observed Ileana dabbing once or twice at her eyes, discreetly.

We walked along the street to the Kino Bar where we discussed the film. Adela held my hand, but there was little warmth in her touch. After a few minutes' necessary silence, Constantin said in his usual slightly pompous manner, "A most interesting film, a most arresting experience." He looked around at us. "There is undeniably much power in it. The theme of the steady and upward advance of science, and its vital inevitability," he went on. "Wells preached scientific progress and the necessity of creating order out of chaos. It all seems very planned and imposed." Constantin is starting his studies in Bucharest soon—as if we couldn't tell! Adela didn't make fun of him as she usually does.

Ileana said quietly, "Yes, we seem to revel in our chaos now, and scientific advance has become frightening or is ignored. But is it a better world than the one that was so painfully reborn in the film?" I said that the film seemed to have had no time for the arts. The arts flourish in a world, in cultures, where there is chaos and uncertainty. That future world was too clean, it was sanitised. Art could therefore only rebel, as it did, against the impositions of science. "The artists in that clean new world had the freedom and leisure in which to pursue their art," Constantin said. "Must the arts only flourish in a chaotic world of war and hate?" He fell silent for a few moments. "I suppose that it is possible that war can bring out great things in people, in nations and cultures. But it also paralyses and retards. It destroys. Like Cabal said in the film, it gets hold of you. I must confess that I feel something of a yearning for that future, clean white world. I feel nostalgia for that future that never was, or could be." When he says things like that I feel Constantin is a true soul-mate, but at other times . . .

Adela said that she had to go. Constantin offered to see her home, as she lives nearer him than me. She agreed, and told me not to bother walking with them. Ileana smiled wanly at me before she ran to catch her tram. What is happening to us? I walked back towards Bucharest Boulevard, and then along and back the length of it several times. It lightened my mood when I realised that the prostitutes along King Carol I Boulevard near Paris Circus might have thought that I was a shy potential customer . . . But I really wasn't interested . . .

The film was still running through my mind when I eventually got home and went to bed. There was no note or phone call from Adela. I dreamed in monochrome, a claustrophobic dream of underground tunnels and chambers, and of crowds in them cowering from air attack. There had been the sense of being weighed down by the city above. There had been an all-pervading sense of terror and helplessness, and, worst of all, a sense of drawn-out duration. I never came out into the sunlit new earth and the clean white city before I woke up.

Monday. I wasn't fit for much at work. Mr. Radulescu noticed and spoke sharply to me a few times. My mind was still focussed far too much on *Things to Come* and my dream. Compared to the book the film is a flawed failure, but its failure is the tragic one of attempted over-achievement and a true vision imperfectly realised. (How I sound like Constantin!) Yet it is a truly magnificent film, and its scope is still immense. It will be praised for decades—if the race can survive the next few years. It is a chilling vision. And how Arthur Bliss's music rings in my ears and still plays in my mind! I must buy it if it is available on records.

Adela was not at home when I called her. I walked around the New Town for hours before I felt like going to bed. I wonder if I will dream again tonight.

Tuesday. I am at home today. I have not been able to go to the office. Last night, or this morning, I dreamed again—at least I think I did. I remember going to bed, thinking of the action and message of the film, and with the music always present. At some point in the middle of the night I got out of bed. My room was stifling, so I went to the window and drew back the curtains. There was no street or moonlight outside. There was only a wasteland, like the blasted areas along the Eastern Front in the Great War that Father told me about. It was as if I was watching another film, but one of that war. Then futuristic tanks, as in *Things to Come*, crawled across the landscape, crushing ruins and what few living things— human and otherwise—that I could see from my vantage-point.

I thought that I was dreaming, watching another film, yet I also knew that I had drawn back the curtains from my bedroom window, and what I was seeing was outside of it. I felt a sick horror and a sense of vertigo. It wasn't to do with height, but time. This war had been going on for decades, as in *Things to Come*. But I wasn't watching a film. Or was I? I don't know. I drew the curtains again and went back to bed. But I soon got up and went to the window again. There was a different scene outside.

The tanks had gone, but a few ruins remained. And people wandered around and through them, poor desperate people who had lost everything. I saw rough buildings grow up against the great stone and concrete remnants of the city. It was like barbarians moving into the ruins of ancient Rome. But these people were not barbarians—they were the survivors, humbled and destitute. I could not tear myself away from my window. Once again, I am not sure when I was dreaming in bed, or when I was really standing at the window, looking out. I know that I am awake now, writing this. It is sunny outside. Or do I still dream?

Time seemed to speed up. The ruined city was rebuilt. Streets and squares covered the devastated landscape. A city of huge towers grew up. Industry was restored. The air was black with smoke and steam. I saw their days and nights flash by. Lurid lights glowed by day and night. Gigantic screens—as in the film—constantly displayed a face that seemed familiar, but which I couldn't place, and which surely had no place in whatever I was seeing. Crowds filled the treeless boulevards and squares, and huddled beneath the screens. I heard Bliss's music from the film, the part when their leader, the Boss, or Chief, returned from one of his campaigns. The music is triumphant, yet full of menace, and the empty glory of totalitarianism and gangsterism. The sky was disturbed. I stumbled back to bed.

Some time later, but when it was still dark, I went yet again to my window. Still the familiar view wasn't there. The city of black towers dominated the landscape, but its crowded streets were empty. For the first time in my dream, or whatever it was, or still is, I could hear the scene. There was a vast subdued roar. I saw a new tower, and it was the tallest of all. And then I saw that it was not a tower. It was like the Space Gun in *Things to Come*. But I knew that there was no-one in it, and that it was not destined for outer space. The crowds that surrounded the colossal barrel were cheering at more great screens erected nearby. The face ranted at them. There was more cheering. The rocket was to be fired for destruction. The screens shut off, like the curtains coming down in the cinema. (At least I can remember that.) People streamed away from the rocket, back to their city. I blinked, and then I saw the city again. It was in ruins. A sea of ruins again. That was all I could see. Where the rocket had been was a gigantic pit. Bliss's desolate music for the ruined landscape and blasted city was in my head. At some point I went back to bed— at least I think so.

Wednesday. Now, I don't know whether I dreamed going in to the office this morning or whether I actually did. Mr. Radulescu and my colleagues never said anything. But I think I could've dreamed much more all at once. At any rate, time seems to have passed, another day in my world. Ileana phoned me to say she thought that Constantin was seeing Adela. I said nothing very much. I walked along by the river and the stadium until I felt tired enough to go back home and sleep. During the night I woke up, but fell asleep again almost immediately. Later I woke up again. It was dark—my curtains were drawn. So I got up and went to the window.

I saw the same vision as before: the ruined, desolate landscape, the decades-long war moving painfully backwards and forwards across it. Again, time sped on. The ruined city was rebuilt. But the vision became a new one. It was closer to the renewed city of *Things to Come*. A city spread out over the landscape, a clean and bright city. And much of it was underground, leaving the surface green and pleasant. The resources of the world reborn after the war were used to create a functional beauty. The world was indeed harvested, but not attacked. Other crowds gathered in vast squares in front of great public screens. The face on the screens was venerable, and worthy of veneration. Another new tower appeared, another "Space Gun", but I knew that it was constructed for science and exploration. The city expanded, but never overflowed its green hills. I drew the curtains and stumbled back to bed.

The next time I woke up I knew that I had really woken up. There was a note from Adela, and it confirmed Ileana's suspicions. Adela was going to Bucharest with Constantin. So I was back in the "real" world all right. My world. Yet how simplistic those words now seem!

Now

Reading those concealed papers had an effect on me: I felt that I could easily have been the author of that document, if I had undergone his experiences. I couldn't explain that, at least not then. I read the account again, and looked through the photographs, turning each one over to look again at any writing on the back. I wanted to find out who the author, the dreamer, was. But there was no indication of his name. There were only his friends' first names; he never gave his own name, and never mentioned their surnames, that foursome who had watched *Things to Come* on that summer afternoon now lost far-off in time. The more I thought about it, the more I wanted to find out who the young man was. He seemed to be a native of Steaua de Munte: perhaps I had even already seen him, one of the very old men sitting in the sun on one of the benches on Star Hill or along by the river. Or perhaps I had been at school with his grandson . . . And there was also the possibility that Mihai Lereanu might be able to help. He might remember who he had got the album from. The Lereanu family had owned bookshops and antique shops in various locations in Steaua de Munte for more years than anyone could remember.

One of the advantages of refurbishing an older structure is that the period appearance can be retained, with the facilities being modernised. When I planned my own apartment, in the main room I'd included the latest and best media entertainment centre available—its modern sleekness hardly contrasted at all with the streamlining of the old windows and mouldings, but it was still different and looked good. And over the years I had accumulated a large collection of classic films on DVD; naturally this included *Things to Come*. I had to watch the film again.

It was dusk when I switched off the screen. A line of lemon-yellow afterglow was painted above the silhouetted rooftops of the town; the white and red towers of the Castle glowed above it, against the darkening sky. As it had before on my frequent viewings, *Things to Come* left an impression on me. I could now understand a little better of what the nameless young man had written. All those years ago he seemed to have been the recipient of multiple visions—a possible heaven and a possible hell, a utopia and a dystopia. And all after a commonplace trip with friends to his local cinema. He watched an important and well-made film. Eventually I began to wonder whether it was possible for there to be something in the experience of watching such a film, with its unparalleled special effects, its music, and its message, that could all come together in such a world and personal situation as he knew, to produce such a range of experiences. Could the cumulative effects somehow break into and through the multiple time-strands of the universes? I felt sure that my man had allowed himself to speculate on such possibilities out of H.G. Wells's fictional probabilities as well—as far as he was able to.

But his ordinary life, his work, friendships, relationships, must have been dominated by more immediate concerns. I knew my history. He had commented on the fact that the cinema showed *Things to Come* in the first place. Did he also have apprehensions and misgivings about such contemporary figures as King Carol II, Codreanu and his Iron Guard, and Admiral Horthy, let alone Hitler, Mussolini, and Stalin? I had formed the impression that my dreamer was a thoughtful young man who contemplated not only the turmoil of his own emotional life, but also the vortex of the powers that be of his time, and wondered what they and their beliefs and policies, their systems, would do to his world. He was emotional and frightened. I felt that the film seemed to have granted him a way of releasing his pent-up feelings.

The next morning I delayed my return to Bucharest so I could visit Lereanu again. I paid for everything that I had taken from the shop. And casually I mentioned the photograph album, but Lereanu knew nothing about its origin. He said it had been jammed into a large box of books that he had brought over from one of his other shops, and it must have been in the back room there for many years.

As I turned to go, Lereanu said, "Hold on, wait a moment. There was one more thing. After you went I noticed this on the floor." He opened a desk drawer and handed me a sealed envelope. It was dusty around the edges, but otherwise clean and undamaged. I immediately noticed that it was addressed to Adela, and was in the young man's handwriting. "It must have fallen out of that photograph album. I assumed you'd want it as well."

I thanked him and took the envelope. I rushed back up to my apartment and put the envelope down on the table next to the photograph album. I felt apprehensive, as if I was standing on the threshold of something unknown. But I had no doubts: I was definitely going to open the envelope. I found my bronze Art Deco paper knife and slit open the envelope. I went out onto the sweeping curve of the terrace and sat down on one of the hard wooden chairs I kept there. I unfolded the sheet of paper—it was proper letter stationery, not torn from a notebook—and smoothed it out. Then I began to read.

When I had finished I paced backwards and forwards along the length of my balcony. I ran one hand along the polished brass rail that had always reminded me of the rail on a ship's deck. The letter was undated and had obviously never been sent to its intended recipient, Adela. I felt sure that he had written this some months, or even years, after the account he had sealed away in the album. Perhaps he had only wanted to write down the final part of the story, to get it out of his system and then shut it away. But then why bother to address the envelope? I do not think that I will ever find out. But he had signed his name to what he had written: Felix.

Felix must have gradually come to terms with the dream or vision he had experienced. He resumed his working life apparently unchanged, except for an inner conviction that the future of the whole world was to be decided very soon. He felt that he had seen a choice of futures—and he could have a part in deciding on one of them, despite his own personal insignificance. He came to think that it had been somehow given to him to be involved in making the crucial choice that would allow one or other of the futures to become tangible reality. Felix was tormented by this imagined responsibility, but he came to see that it was in continuing to do his daily work, and living his humdrum existence, which would make all the difference—for the good. The echoing last words he wrote were: "All or nothing? Which is it to be? All or nothing?"

I had no idea how Felix thought he would recognise and enable the vital divergence, to allow the clean white world to become a reality. There was no clue as to the time-scale. Sitting in the fresh breeze out on my balcony, it felt to me that the walls were insubstantial and hazy; and for a moment I looked out and over my world as through a heat haze. I could not help but think: Which world are we in? Which future? Are we on the way to utopia—or what? I would give anything to know. As I stood there, in another part of the same building where Felix had watched the film that had stirred his vision—or delusion—I thought: Did he make the right choice? Could the fact that I was here, on site, be the reason I was being affected so much? And what inadvertent part was I playing?

Back at work in Bucharest, the questions and possibilities haunted me as I thought about what to do next. Now I knew my mystery man's name was Felix, I had something to go on. I had some photographs; and with a name I could hope to rouse memories. That took several weeks. At weekends I travelled back to Steaua de Munte and made enquiries in the town museum and with organisations for very old people. I asked my parents to try to remember if they had heard my grandparents ever mention anything. I posted the photographs on the internet, on a special web page I created.

At times I was convinced that I would never find out what I wanted to know. Luckily I was always busy and disciplined enough at work to keep a sense of proportion; but at times, as when I was on my own in my lovely modernist apartment, I found it difficult to imagine ever coming to the end of what had become some sort of a quest for me. I read books and documents about the era Felix lived in, and thoroughly explored the dark paths that the modern history of my own country had sometimes taken. But we had emerged into sunlight at long last, hadn't we?

Perhaps that was the hope that anyone living through the monochrome horrors, such as were depicted in the film, yearned and cried out for in his very being. Were those hopes really there? Were they there for anyone to attain? Or had they always been too late? Was everyone too late? At that time everything was in the balance—everything. The sunlit streamlined Moderne future or the new dark age. All or nothing . . .

There is little more to add. Recently I came into possession of Felix's surname. My mother had died, and when my father and I went through her papers we found an old school exercise book that she had used to write phone numbers and shopping lists in. The first few pages had been neatly cut out; the name Felix, with surname, was written on the inside front cover in handwriting I had come to recognise as much as my own. I had no recollection of ever seeing the book before. My father said that as far as he knew, my mother had used it since they were married; her mother could well have given it to her, or she could have bought it for a few lei in a junk shop. My mother always had an eye for economies and would never waste even a single scrap of paper.

I continued my enquiries in Steaua de Munte, Sibiu, throughout Transylvania, and Bucharest—anywhere I thought that information about Felix could be found. But no. He seems to have vanished. Of course, there had been plenty of opportunities over the decades. Perhaps he was a victim of the Iron Guard, or had been one of the many inhabitants of German ancestry deported in 1945 to the Soviet Union, suspected of collaborating with the recently overthrown fascist regime of Ion Antonescu. If he had been deported, there was no record either of his departure—or return, if he ever had come back. Perhaps he had emigrated, or maybe his papers had simply been misfiled somewhere, and he is still alive and well, but untraceable. And perhaps that is the way he wants it to be, and how it should be. So I do not know exactly what happened—or what might yet happen, although I can dream. As I hope that everyone can—in the right way. I still hope that much.

And one small normal thing I could do, before too much longer, is to arrange with the Cinema Cosmopolitain to show *Things to Come* again . . .

In Strange Earth

Tudor Brănescu could not believe what he was seeing. He had switched on his television to watch the Leader's speech being broadcast live from the Central Committee Building in Palace Square. If he was at home, that always seemed to be the safest thing to do. As a teenager he had watched while the Leader condemned the Soviet invasion of Czechoslovakia in 1968 from the same balcony overlooking the same square; everyone had praised him, and Brănescu had been pleased and proud to be growing up in a country under such inspired and courageous leadership. But now . . .

Brănescu had come to serve the Leader well. He studied hard at school and university, and took part with devotion when the students had to help to gather in the harvest or work on the road to the great dam being built high in the Carpathians. In Bucharest he became active in the Party, and got himself noticed by his superiors, but not so much so that they could ever feel threatened. On one occasion Brănescu was watching a small, ancient brick church being surrounded with scaffolding before it was to be moved a few metres, to make way for one of the great roads with which the Leader wished to improve the capital city. At the time, Brănescu wondered why the crumbling building was not simply demolished—after all, enough others had been, and more would undoubtedly follow—but if it had been decided that the church was to be moved, then that's all there was to it. Brănescu knew that his parents and grandparents, if they had still been alive, would have wished it. He always kept his parents' views to himself, never talking about them to his friends, even after a night of drinking and smoking with them.

He stood near the reprieved church, gradually moving closer and closer to it so he could get a better view of the great hydraulic mechanisms that were to raise the building. A large black limousine drove up and disgorged the Mayor of his Sector. Brănescu knew him by sight. The Mayor and his cronies strode across to where the foreman and engineers were making the final preparations to begin the lifting process. Brănescu moved even closer to where they were standing, by the tarpaulin-shrouded porch. He heard the orders being given to start the machinery, and the engineers' protests that they were not quite ready yet. Nevertheless, after a few minutes, the engines were started. Brănescu looked with wonder as the entire building shuddered and moved; a terrifying memory of the last great earthquake came and went, mercifully briefly. Then there was a sudden movement above them, and Brănescu instinctively jumped to his right as several bricks slid loose from the porch and showered down, bringing powdery mortar and brick dust with them. His time working at the bottom of the almost vertically-sided valleys near the dam project had not been wasted. He cannoned into the Mayor, and bystanders shouted in panic, perhaps thinking that the mayor was being attacked. The two men hit the ground and rolled away as the bricks fell to earth just where the Mayor had been standing. As they got up and dusted themselves down, a bodyguard advanced towards Brănescu. The Mayor waved him away. "Where were you?" he shouted at him. "Where were you? It was this young comrade who saved me."

From that day on, the Mayor kept Brănescu near him at all times. He was given a tiny room of his own in one of the new blocks, and learnt to drive the Mayor's car, although he was not the chauffeur. Brănescu was not a bodyguard, although he was usually placed close to his new employer as if he were one. Ion Lereanu, who actually was a bodyguard, befriended Brănescu and helped him to find his way through the complex web of patronage and shifting alliances that seemed to count for so much. Brănescu grew to like Lereanu and to feel that he could genuinely trust him: a feeling that he seemed to reciprocate, as Lereanu told his new friend about his parents and grandparents, and about growing up in a small ancient town in remote Transylvania.

Sometimes Brănescu was allowed to sit at the Mayor's table and enjoy a wealth of delicacies that almost everyone else had forgotten existed: steaks, bananas, grapes, cream cakes. Brănescu was with the Mayor when the Leader himself bestowed personal favour and promoted him. Soon the former Mayor was heavily involved with the planning and construction of the Palace of the People. The Leader and his wife, the Mother of the Nation, were always visiting the site and the design offices, and Brănescu was always there in the background. Brănescu appeared in the background of so many official photographs that even he heard the rumour that he really worked for the Leader himself. The wilder rumours said that Brănescu was a distant relative of the Leader or the Mother of the Nation, or even an illegitimate child. As the years passed, Brănescu came to the conclusion that he was regarded as some sort of mascot or human good-luck charm to be kept around, useless but necessary. And, of course, only worth keeping while the luck held. Nevertheless, he made the best of his privileged position, after all, it could have all been so much worse. In his heart Brănescu knew that somehow he had sold himself. But he was never sure what for.

That dank Thursday morning Brănescu was glad that he hadn't been "invited" to go and join the crowd in Palace Square, even though he would have had an exalted position at the front. It was a cold and grey morning, and it would not have been pleasant to be standing around in the open air listening to a long speech, waving flags, cheering, and applauding strictly on cue. Brănescu felt that even had he been wedged into the square with the hundred thousand other people filling it, their combined body heat together with the hot air that would no doubt blow down from the balcony, would have made no difference, and he would still have been shivering.

The Leader started on his prepared speech, as expected condemning the uprising in Timişoara. When the Leader moved on to praise his regime's achievements, Brănescu mentally tuned out well-used phrases and concentrated on watching the grainy picture. Huddled in his little room, he thought of the large, ornately furnished and lavishly equipped rooms that the Leader and his wife had come from that morning, and to which they would no doubt go back to. Brănescu's attention wandered, but he came back to himself again with a start when he realised that the applause was nothing like as widespread as it should have been. There even seemed to be some booing. The Leader faltered in his speech. The camera moved away from the figure on the balcony, and panned along the façades of other buildings in Palace Square, catching their rooflines and the sky. Then Brănescu heard someone tapping the microphone and calling "Hello, hello", as if he was a technician testing a faulty connection. Then the Leader reappeared, waving jerkily, like a puppet whose control was being lost. By now his wife's voice was audible as well.

Brănescu thought the performance was on the way to be-coming even more farcical than usual. The row of old men in heavy overcoats and hats stood on the balcony like stat-ues, until the Mother of the Nation started to lead them in clapping and slogans, as if they could drown out the noise of the tens of thousands of people below. The crowd now threatened to transform into a mob at any moment, but Brănescu was shocked to see that the Leader didn't seem to recognise that. Trying to make himself heard over the crowd's booing and jeering, the Leader started to an-nounce pay rises and pension increases. The camera cut away to reveal the crowd. Then it sharply returned to the Leader on his balcony, as he seemed to recover his stride and continued with his litany of pay increases. All his lengthening string of sentences seemed to be ending with the word "lei" as if he was casting a spell. The Leader's wife gestured for quiet, but it was not working. With incredu-lity Brănescu heard the crowd chanting "Down with the dictator!" The Leader hesitated again, and finally stopped speaking. The broadcast was cut.

Brănescu gazed at the screen, in horrified fascination as the broadcast resumed, showing the chaos to be seen by the millions of people watching it across the country. He tore himself away from the screen and went over to the window. Freezing winter air poured in, but Brănescu kept the win-dow open long enough to be able to hear what sounded like chanting and shouting in the distance. And shooting.

There was a hammering at his door. "Comrade Brănescu! Mr. Brănescu!" It was his neighbour, Mrs. Ralea. He opened the door. "Have you seen it?" she shouted. "What's going on? They're shooting. The Leader is trapped in the Central Committee Building. It's terrible. I've heard the Securitate are shooting people to restore order in Pal-ace Square! Why don't they do more to help?"

Brănescu slammed the door in her face and rushed back to the window. Mrs. Ralea banged on the door a few more times, but stomped off down the corridor and started banging on other doors. Leaning out, Brănescu was certain that he could hear scattered gunfire, but behind it the low swelling sound of a riot, like the tide flooding in over a shingle beach, was unmistakeable. He shut the window and drew the curtains and sat next to the television set, switching it off. He did not want to be here in his apartment, but he remembered that he could have been in the Central Committee Building, waiting for the speech to end so he could join in the usual applause and give the Leader and the Mother of the Nation the usual adulation. He had been lucky. But the Leader's luck had finally run out first. Brănescu knew he had to leave, to get away from Bucharest.

He decided to wait until nightfall. In the meantime he gathered together all the money he could find, and his papers, and stuffed them into the inside pocket of his warmest coat. He sat in the chair, trying to keep warm, and not to make a sound. Twice there was knocking at his door, but each time he ignored it, and it eventually stopped. Even with the window closed Brănescu heard occasional shooting and shouting, with vehicles being driven at high speed through the city. He thought about how he could reach the garage containing the large black limousine that he sometimes drove as chauffeur, but settled for imagining getting away in an inconspicuous Dacia, if he could find one there, incongruous amongst the other vehicles. He must be lucky for himself and find one there.

As the night deepened, Brănescu's luck had held, even as he tried not to think any more of the luck of his presumably erstwhile employers. He had no problem getting into the garage; his identity card got him past the solitary guard who had remained at his post. The guard had asked no questions. And there were a couple of grimy and mud-spattered Dacias still waiting to be cleaned. Brănescu chose the older one and made sure that the petrol tank was full. He grabbed some full cans of petrol and laid them down in the back of the car.

Once back outside, Brănescu drove as fast as he could without drawing attention to himself. He avoided the boulevards and other main roads, and threaded his way along side roads and wove through housing estates, aiming to join the main road heading north-west towards Piteşti. As he drove he turned over possibilities in his mind: where to go until everything had calmed down again, and what to do then. Brănescu did not doubt that order would be restored, but he thought it was quite possible that the Leader's time had come at last. Someone else could well emerge on top; and if he could be as far away as possible, Brănescu hoped that the Leader—old or new—might forget about him in all the chaos.

As dawn came, the dull and overcast sky stretched above him mirroring the flat countryside he was driving through. He had left Bucharest behind. Sometimes convoys of trucks full of soldiers sped past him, heading towards the city, and Brănescu drove as far away as he could from them, respectfully keeping his distance like a good comrade should. Once in Piteşti, he realised how hungry and thirsty he was. Along the main avenue most of the shops were open, and Brănescu parked the car and wandered along until he found a supermarket. Luck was on his side, and there wasn't much of a queue.

Brănescu came away with a loaf of bread and a bottle of watery orange juice. As he was opening the door of his car, a man walked over to him.

"What's happening in Bucharest? We watched the television, and he was going to speak again, but it's all gone again. The phones start working but stop again. We're hearing so many rumours."

"What makes you think I know anything?"

The man laughed. "You're not from around here. Your car, or rather the car you're driving, has Bucharest number plates. Something's going on, isn't it? I was told that they're shooting in the streets, and flags are being flown with the Party emblem ripped out of them."

Brănescu forced himself to smile. "Yes, I'm driving out from Bucharest. But I didn't see anything. I heard some firing, but that was all. I need to get going, I've got to get to my mother. She's seriously ill. Probably dying."

The man stepped back. "I won't keep you then, Comrade. Have a safe journey. Where are you heading to?"

"Transylvania—Sibiu," Brănescu answered, naming the first town on the other side of the mountains that came into his mind.

"As I said, I wish you a safe journey—to Sibiu."

Brănescu drove away as fast as he could. He hadn't given any thought as to his final destination, only to get away from Bucharest and over the mountains. Sibiu might do as well as anywhere. Then he remembered that the Leader's elder son was Party chief there. Sibiu might not be such a good idea after all. As he drove, Brănescu thought about other towns he had driven to, or visited when he had been a part of the entourage. Sighişoara might be a possibility, or Steaua de Munte. Of course, that was the town that Ion Lereanu had always talked about. "It is a special sort of place, Tudor," he had told him. And Brănescu remembered that he had liked Steaua de Munte. The Leader had stayed in a magnificent room in the old castle, high on a hill above the town on one side and the river on the other. The castle had been restored and refurbished; even the rooms where the bodyguards and drivers were assigned had been freshly decorated and furnished. From the window Brănescu had been able to see across the old town to another, lower hill at the opposite end of the main street that linked them. Ion had told him that his father and grandfathers had often spoken about how brightly-lit the boulevards had been before the War. "Parisville, that part of town was called," he had said. "Like a smaller version of the Little Paris itself, Bucharest. At least the Old Town isn't being swept away. It's going to be restored, for the tourists. The foreigners love all that stuff. I'm pleased too. Steaua de Munte is—special. That's all I can say. A good place."

A good place. The phrase went round and round in Brănescu's head as he drove. That was all he wanted to find. Surely it was not too much to hope for: a good place.

Soon he was approaching Curtea de Argeş. Seeing the name made Brănescu remember an old history book that Ion had once carefully shown him. The first king and queen of Romania were buried there, in the cathedral. All he knew about that king was that he had ordered the bloody suppression of a peasants' revolt. Brănescu had once driven his patron to Curtea de Argeş for a Party rally. One of the local leaders had spoken about the town's great history and its steadfast people, and how it had become Wallachia's capital, and the nation had sprung from its union with Moldavia, and how the future would soon equal— and actually outshine by far—that illustrious past . . . But nobody had mentioned the royal tombs or the church and monastery. Brănescu wondered if he could stop in Curtea de Argeş and try and find the cathedral. He remembered the pictures in Ion's book, and wondered if he could pray there, perhaps at the royal tombs themselves . . . Ion had mentioned praying once, but . . . Brănescu had never been taught to pray, but thought that he could learn, given time. Nourished from somewhere deep within he imagined ranks of glowing candles, the piercing eyes of robed mosaic saints, with the Pantokrator above all, hand raised in a stern blessing. He smelt incense and heard the voices of priests and a chanting choir. Sometimes it sounded like "Tudor . . . Tudor . . . " Brănescu stood in the warm dimness, one hand resting on a pillar, as worshippers came and went all around him. Lights flickered and the air grew pleasantly thick . . .

A horn blaring out brought Brănescu back to reality, and he swerved to avoid a truck coming towards him. He thought that he must have almost fallen asleep. But for one more moment the chilly grey December day, which already seemed to be losing itself in an early twilight, was replaced again by a dream of tall domes lost in the holy gloom of centuries rising high over him, before it was gone. Brănescu drove on, straight through Curtea de Argeş and towards the high pass over the mountains.

The road ascended slowly, constantly doubling back on itself as it gained height. Trees had given way to steep and rough rocky pasture, empty of sheep this late in the year. The only buildings Brănescu had seen since crossing the dam at Lake Vidraru were unfinished tourist cabins, and a small hotel closed for the winter. There had been few cars heading in either direction. The sky cleared, and by late afternoon he had reached the pass. He stopped the car and got out for a moment, looking back and down, the way he had come. The highest peaks were still sunlit, but the tens of kilometres of country falling away behind him were lost in darkness and shadow. Brănescu drove on through the short tunnel that bored its way under the last ridge of the mountains.

Brănescu decided not to attempt to reach Steaua de Munte that night. His arms were trembling with the tension of driving, and he was also weak with fatigue. Yet above all he needed to stay awake on the long winding road down into Transylvania. Eventually the road passed through beech woods, and Brănescu drove off the road and onto a patch of firm and dry ground under the trees, darker still than the inky star-spattered sky above. He fell asleep as soon as he had switched off the engine.

On the outskirts of Sibiu, Brănescu found a café and was able to buy some rolls and a cracked mug of a hot liquid that was sold to him as coffee. He had avoided the town centre, because he felt certain that someone might have recognised him if he had walked the streets. He had done so enough times in the past, as one of the name-less group far back in the entourage of the Leader or of one of the others; too unknown to be noticed, but not too unnoticeable never to be forgotten. And never to-tally ignored—just in case. In the café there was a small television set resting on the counter. Bucharest was still in turmoil, with rioting and shooting going on in most other cities throughout the country. One of the men in the café advised Brănescu to eat up and drive on quickly; Sibiu was quiet that morning, but the Party offices had been stormed, and the Leader's son was nowhere to be found, and maybe the army or Securitate were planning a counterattack. Then they watched the television again. It was now confirmed that the Leader and his wife had fled Bucharest by helicopter, flushed out of hiding and chased away. Crowds were demonstrating in Palace Square, wav-ing flags with holes in them. "We've got our country back again," the man whispered. "If they'll let us keep it." Brănescu finished his coffee and left the café.

The two hills gradually became visible in the distance, and slowly resolved themselves into the scene. Steaua de Munte: one hill crowned by its white and red castle, its towers sticking up like fingers pointing at the sun;

the other empty, like the matted bare back of an animal crouching over the town. A few factories and apartment blocks were scattered, seemingly at random, by the river to the south and east of the town. Reaching Bucharest Boulevard, Brănescu drove along until he found a place to park the car, under a leafless tree with a rusty Art Nouveau lamp-post standing next to it. Shops were mostly open, but empty. He noticed a few jagged pieces of glass glinting on the pavement; there were the black marks of burning in one of the empty parking spaces. Yet the town seemed quiet and still under the tall and empty sky. The sun was over in the west, and caught windows in the castle, turning them into drops of molten gold hanging against crisp white walls.

Brănescu wandered into the Old Town, through Market Square and into Central Square past the Lutheran church. He should be looking for somewhere to stay for the night, but he wanted to walk in the open air. Brănescu stumbled; the pavement was uneven, and the cobbles of the centre of the street did not look much safer. He looked down where he walked, but he could not tear his eyes away from the roofs of the old houses glowing in the low golden sun, contrasting with the faded and peeling pastel walls of the houses falling into deepening shadow. He wandered through the twilight, as a few meagre lights started to come on in the rooms behind bleary windows. Soon he found himself standing in front of a gate in the town wall. Although there were a few cars and trucks driving past, he could hear the rushing noise of falling water—a river must be nearby. A few minutes later Brănescu stood at the side of a street overlooking the river, flowing fast and black in the gloom. Flecks of white foam showed there was a weir. There seemed to be a man fishing there, hunched up against a block of stone at the bottom of the slope running down from the street. Brănescu peered at the shape and coughed loudly, but the man didn't move.

Brănescu crossed a narrow bridge. A sign, cemented into the tower of a baroque church, pointed the way to the railway station. The church was in darkness. He pushed at the door, but it was firmly locked. Again, he wanted to try to pray, but none of the buildings built for that seemed to be available to him. He turned back. The man was still huddled by the weir. Brănescu picked his way carefully down a narrow flight of steps to the narrow quay where the man was. Only one of the streetlights along the road above him was working. In the dimness Brănescu gently said, "Good evening." The man did not reply or move. Brănescu patted him on the shoulder. The material of his coat felt sticky. Pulling his hand away, Brănescu saw the dampness black against his pale skin. The body curled up into itself, as if it was still alive and was trying to escape the touch of a concerned friend. The face made itself invisible to him; he thought of Ion Lereanu, his friend. Perhaps he had also escaped from Bucharest, and had come home.

Brănescu rubbed his hands against the rough stone and left the body where it was. The street by the river was deserted, but he wouldn't have called attention to the dead man anyway, even if it had really been Ion. That sharp thought pained Brănescu more than he still thought possible, and he slammed the door shut on it, adding it to all the others. He walked back past the church, but it was still locked. Now he did need to find somewhere to stay. Although Steaua de Munte was very quiet now, who knows what might happen during the night? And a stranger walking the streets would surely not be permitted . . .

Back within the town walls, Brănescu eventually found himself in another square. Lights built out from the walls of houses burned dimly, and he saw a narrow passageway leading to a guesthouse. The proprietor was hardly interested in his guest, as his gaze kept returning to the television on his desk. Brănescu's money helped the process along. "They've lost the Leader and Her," he said, as he handed Brănescu the key to his room. "Can you believe it? They've lost them."

In his room Brănescu thought about what the proprietor had said. Not that the Leader had escaped, or had vanished, presumed lost, but that he had *been* lost, as if the country itself or the people were somehow responsible. If we think that, we all deserve to be as lost as I am, he thought. His dreams were all of movement and pursuit, and of seeking sanctuary. He ran up and down Expressionist streets and hammered on doors. The only doors that opened to him were churches or synagogues; in the dream it was uncertain. Curtains parted in front of a great arch, revealing an iconostasis which slid down into the floor. A muddy road stretched out in front of him, with two elderly people in overcoats and hats threading their way slowly along, trying to avoid mud and puddles. The old couple were holding hands; the woman kept up a constant low muttering, unmistakeably of complaint and self-pity. Brănescu overtook them, and the man called out: "Tudor!" It was the Leader, together with the Mother of the Nation: fleeing, wandering, abandoned. Brănescu shook his head and trudged on past them. "I must get home, get home . . . " he repeated, as the flat grey plains swelled up and met the sky and swallowed them.

The next morning when he had finished his coffee, Brănescu asked the proprietor if he knew anyone called Lereanu.

"There used to be a Lereanu's Bookshop on Mediaş Street, near the town museum," he replied. "But it's been closed for years. I never knew what became of the family. Why do you ask?"

Without giving a clear answer, Brănescu buttoned up his coat and went out. He bought a newspaper, but that told him nothing new. Then he asked for a town map and was offered a small booklet of blurred photographs, which included a map folded into the back cover.

"It's mainly the German tourists buy these," Brănescu was told. "They come back looking for where they came from, as if leaving wasn't good enough for them. Here, look." The shopkeeper opened the brochure and pointed to the map. "It even calls Steaua de Munte 'Sternberg-stadt'—the old Saxon name. I thought we'd done away with all that years ago. And some of the street names are in German too." He laughed and handed the booklet over. "But we never got rid of many of the signs in the Old Town anyway, can you beat that? We never really changed much, not here. And them in Bucharest and Sibiu ignored us for years."

Brănescu ambled through the Old Town, wandering up and down narrow streets and passages. As he had been told, most of the old street signs were in German and Magyar; sometimes there were newer (although still often with the paint worn and flaked) signs in Romanian. Or the Romanian name had been painted on the wall under the original one, and clearly renewed time after time. He wondered about trying to find Ion, or a member of his family. He thought about the dead man by the river. He suddenly found he had left the network of narrow streets and alleys behind him. He was standing at the edge of a wide, curving street, slicing through the Old Town; Sinaia Boulevard, according to the map. There was further evidence that there had been some disturbances: a car had been burnt out and some shop windows smashed. There were bullet marks in the walls. Brănescu wondered when all this had happened; all around him Steaua de Munte

seemed ordinary even if a little subdued. He followed the
street out of the ancient area bounded by the town wall.
People walked past him, averting their gaze or looking
down at their feet, and Militia vehicles mingled with ordinary cars. No-one took any notice of him.

Mediaş Street followed the edge of a small bedraggled
park. The town museum was on the far side of a paved
area. Brănescu walked over to the museum, thinking that
it would be an ideal place to ask about the Lereanu family,
but the door was locked. The museum looked as if it had
been neglected for years. Further along Mediaş Street was
a block of shops; none of them was a bookshop or showed
any sign of ever having been one. He asked passers-by
about it, harassed women on their way to or from queues,
but none of them claimed to have ever heard of anyone
named Lereanu.

Ion had been the only friend that Brănescu had ever
known. Surely he would come back to Steaua de Munte
if he knew his friend Tudor had also gone there in his
hour of need. The two young men had enjoyed their time
together when they had stayed in the castle. For a day or
so, a mere few hours, they had almost been on holiday.
Brănescu consulted his map, although he could see Castle
Hill from where he stood. He walked fast along Bucharest
Boulevard, hands deep in his coat pockets and keeping his
head down, not wanting to have to look anyone in the eye.
He walked past his Dacia, following the wide street as it
skirted the town wall. Brănescu turned along another avenue, not as wide as Bucharest Boulevard, and walked on
through a gate, regaining the Old Town within its circling
walls. He remembered that it had not been possible to
drive to the top of Castle Hill: everyone, even the dignitaries, had had to walk up the great curve of broad, shallow
stone steps that wound up and around the slope of the hill

from the square at its foot. "You should have these steps smoothed out," the Mayor had been told, but nothing had been done.

The houses fell away behind and below him as Brănescu mounted the steps. Soon he was higher than the great town wall, with its wide walkway. Here the river skirted the base of Castle Hill and the wall, both dropping vertically into the black water that slid by so fast and so silently. As he trudged up the steps, Brănescu saw washed-out fields, and mountains mist-shrouded in the distance. New suburbs began on the other side of the river, with apartment blocks and factory chimneys poking up above leafless trees and low rooftops. He reached the baroque gateway that he remembered, set in the far older fortifications surrounding it.

"Castle's closed," the gatekeeper told him, but the man stepped back and let Brănescu walk through and into the courtyard anyway. There was another courtyard on the other side of the castle, with a garden and a small lawn, where the Castle Church stood, its gothic pinnacles soaring skywards. Memories of that day he had spent here before were coming back to him. The main entrance to the church was reached by a narrow pavement, with nothing except a parapet of carved stone battlements and covered benches between it and the almost vertical side of the hill falling away hundreds of feet into the river. He had walked around the outside of the church and along the path with Ion; the vaulted porch was sheltered from the wind, and they sat there in the sun, the ancient stone of the seats warm against the palms of their hands. They did not enter the vast church. After what seemed a long time, Ion had said, "Do you ever pray, Tudor?" Brănescu had laughed, and the moment he'd opened his mouth he wished that the blocks of stone surrounding them would have swallowed the sound, his unthought reaction to feelings thatß he had hardly dared to consider. But there was no going back. Ion opened his mouth and closed it again; for a moment he looked as if he'd been slapped in the face. Brănescu hadn't spoken or moved, although he was crying out to, inside. Ion had got up and ran his hand over the massive lock of the great door, just for a moment. He did not try to pull up the handle and turn it. All he had said was, "Let's go back down." Ion had never looked Brănescu in the eye again, not once, before he was transferred shortly afterwards.

Sitting in the same place again, Brănescu fought back tears, blowing his nose on his handkerchief, as if the gargoyles high up on the walls were observing him and taking notes on his weakness. He gazed out over the river, and then followed the path further along, where he and Ion had never had the chance to walk. The way followed the edge of the hill, curving round to meet the castle on the other side of the church. Ornately carved mullioned openings looked down on the Old Town, a mass of streets and houses flowing around the base of the lower and broader Star Hill. Brănescu turned away and wandered through the main gate again and back down the steps into the town.

From a brick gateway in Star Square a flight of steps led straight up to the top of Star Hill. They were sheltered by a wooden roof, like the steps that led up to the church and hillside cemetery in Sighişoara. In Steaua de Munte, Star Hill was the old town graveyard as well. At the top Brănescu opened the iron gates and stepped into the cemetery. He wandered along the paths between the gravestones and tombs. Sometimes he stopped by a cracked and overgrown stone and knelt down, brushing away dead leaves twigs to read the inscription. "*Ruht in fremder Erde, er hat es Gott gewollt . . .*" Brănescu whispered the words to himself; he imagined a man out of place in strange and alien soil. But no soil could ever be alien if there were the warm memories of association. On the far side of the town Castle Hill and its buildings dominated the skyline; the gulf between, separating Brănescu from the scene of what he now realised was his life's failure, was unbridgeable and absolute. There was no going back—he walked around and around in a quiet place of rest and death.

On the opposite side of Star Hill, the vast open space of Republic Square stretched from the outer boulevard to the base of the hill. Decades earlier a section of the town wall had been torn down to make way for it. Brănescu remembered that Ion had told him that there were those in the town who held that breaching the wall allowed an undesirable mixing of something indefinable from within the walls outside, also compromising the "apartness" of Star Hill. Two worlds that should scarcely meet were in constant flux together. Brănescu could not return to one world; perhaps the other remained to him. He slumped down on a wooden bench overlooking the square. It was almost empty, although as he watched, groups of people, tiny figures far below, were drifting into the square from all directions. The town Party Office occupied a large grey modernist block on the side of Republic Square opposite Star Hill, and Brănescu saw that it had been damaged. Several windows were missing glass, and gaped open, black against the pale walls. The walls themselves were smoke-stained in places. A flag flew as usual, but it had the emblem ripped out of its centre. A crowd was gathering in front of the building, and a group of people came out onto the balcony. With a shock Brănescu was reminded of the scenes he had watched on his television, high up in his tiny apartment in Bucharest, only a couple of days ago but already in a different era. The sounds of cheering and clapping drifted up in the cold air; the crowd was celebrating.

Perhaps the Leader had been found and restored to power, his luck having changed and everything in the world falling back into accustomed place.

Brănescu shook his head and closed his eyes, but instead of seeing swirling streamers of colour against the darkness, he saw the old couple still forlornly wandering the lanes and streets of the country. Still hand in hand, they drifted away into the distance, the expanse of grass and concrete growing between them and Brănescu's shrinking viewpoint. A few shots rang out over the town, and there was more cheering. Brănescu opened his eyes, and Ion was standing in front of him, looking directly at him and smiling. Brănescu smiled back and got to his feet, stretching out his arms, but Ion did not move as Brănescu stumbled past and through him. Something had changed for him. Brănescu sat down again, and thought about going down from the heights of Star Hill and returning home to Bucharest. Perhaps he would meet Ion there after all, but he didn't really believe that. It wasn't necessary now, any more than leaving the cemetery really was. Nevertheless . . . As the day wore on, Brănescu remained sitting there. It was a good place.

The Silver Voice

Thus the stranger trembles in darkness
As he softly raises his eyelids over a human shape
Far away; the silver voice of the wind in the hallway.

                              – Georg Trakl (1887-1914)

"The Windowless Room" by Alexandru Neascu

In a house on a certain square, in the city of S———, there was a room with no windows. Foursquare, an exact cube in its dimensions, it was located in the very centre of the house, and could only be entered through a door to which Z., the owner of the house, possessed the only key. The walls and ceiling of the windowless room were sheathed with thin sheets of palely veined marble; the floor was paved with marble of the purest white. And inlaid into the floor in copper, tinted green with verdigris, was an outline of the borders of the Greater Romanian State: to Z. the most beautiful Form. And that Form was kept entirely covered with a darker green carpet woven through with a gridwork of silver threads. A single lamp set in the centre of each wall, equidistant from each corner, the floor and ceiling, provided all the light required. In the centre of the room stood an ebony table, on which a small iron box, manufactured to exact specifications and patterned with raised intersecting lines, precisely placed. The box was not locked; there was no requirement for that.

Z. was certain that no-one but him knew about the windowless room. The architect who had designed the room at the behest of Z. had died. The workmen whom the architect had employed to make the room a reality had been sworn to secrecy, and then, one by one, within six months, had also died in a variety of ways. Z. lived and worked alone in the house. He entered the windowless room as often as he had necessity and desire to; and the years went by in S——, and Z. remained. The windowless room awaited the greater purpose for which it had been intended.

And a Movement rose up throughout the land, a Movement dedicated to achieving the long awaited revival of the Nation and a new Romania. This was the aim of all its efforts, struggle, and sacrifice. And Z. was glad and he knew that the reason for the creation of the windowless room was being fulfilled. Peasants and students, intellectuals and factory workers rallied to the Movement, and prepared to cleanse their country, and renew and redeem themselves in blessed sacrifice even unto death.

Z. walked through the antique streets of the town of S——. He ascended its twin hills and circled its walls. He passed under each of the town's seven ancient gates and crossed and crossed again its river bridges. He circumnavigated the town through the networks of boulevards and squares, the new districts of apartment blocks and factories in the outer suburbs.

The fortunes of the Movement waxed and waned. Z. would enter the windowless room, locking the door behind him, and stand by the ebony table. With one hand resting on the top of the iron box, he would push his palm hard down on it until he could feel the design of the raised lines being pressed into his skin. When the troubles came and the Chief gave himself to the Nation in death, Z. performed the first invocation. And then, as hundreds were allowed to experience merciful death, the second. Rolling back the carpet Z. gazed on the Form inlaid into the pure white marble of the floor. And the Form was the colour of the pale dawning fire of the rose.

The next invocation was performed at the climax of the summer of the Great Catastrophe. The copper-bounded Form was changed: shrunken, distorted from its former beauty; the marble not red enough.

And the Movement finally achieved power and Z. travelled to the Capital to join the celebrations and to pledge himself again to the wedding with death to which he had been called. And many were called, and many chosen; and Z. returned to the town of S——, his work and his vigils and invocations in the central room that had no windows.

And the Movement rose up and dear death was visited upon it; but the martyrs caused the blood of the Movement's enemies to drown them.

Z. invoked the glorious dead, who still lived because they were a part of the Nation. And his palms smarted with the touch of the cold ridged iron of the box on the black table for the last time; and Z. extinguished the four lamps for the last time; and he gazed at the great Form, now displayed in the full bright ruby red of blood against the white marble. He locked the door to the windowless room. Moonlight shone through the great round-headed window at the front of the house, casting shadows over the sweeping staircase and hall. As the bells chimed the hour from the yellow and white tower of the church on the corner, Z. departed from his house and the town of S—— forever.

I arrived back at the office in the late afternoon. I had driven straight from Oradea, and all I intended to do was to check my post and then go on home for the weekend. A small pile of mail from that morning had been left on my desk, and I flipped through the envelopes in case there was something that couldn't wait until Monday. At the bottom of the heap was a padded envelope bearing American stamps with a Chicago postmark; as I turned it over I couldn't think of anyone there who would be writing to me. I didn't recognise the firm but somewhat uneven handwriting on the front of the envelope, and there was no return address. Curiosity got the better of me. As the contents slid clear, out of the protective padding, I smelt the unique aroma of old newsprint paper. I held a slim booklet, cheaply produced, clearly fragile and beginning to disintegrate. The staples were rusted, and the edges of some of the pages were crumbling; a light confetti of fragments showered onto my desk. I had never heard of *The Martyr*—but I was thoroughly familiar with the symbol that dominated the cover. It was the Triple Cross of the Legion of the Archangel Michael—the Iron Guard. The drawing surrounding the Legion's emblem was of a book open at a map of Greater Romania in the midst of a stylised rolling landscape of trees, meadows, and rivers, with mountains in the distance and swirling clouds above. I put the pamphlet down on my desk and opened it carefully. The first page was a table of contents, followed by an introduction. Judging by this, *The Martyr* appeared to be an anthology of stories and poems by and for members of the Iron Guard.

I shook the envelope out over my desk, but nothing else fell out except for some more fragments of paper. There was no letter, nothing to tell me why someone in the United States had sent me this particular old booklet. I gently slid it back into the envelope and put it in my briefcase. Then I left the office and walked back out into

King Carol I Boulevard, trying not to think about one of the names I had just seen on the contents page: Alexandru Neascu. My name.

The old boulevards and squares of Steaua de Munte have been beautifully restored; the bulky Art Nouveau and Moderne hybrid that is the Hotel Paris is once again the place to go for people who want to be at the centre of things in the town. Normally on a Friday evening I would go to one of the bars there and meet friends and colleagues, discuss the highlights of the working week just gone by and talk about plans for the weekend. But this time I walked quickly around Paris Circus, ignoring the hotel, and along Sinaia Boulevard where I rented a superb apartment in a newly renovated building far along the great curve of the street, almost at Star Square. The boulevard's length seemed interminable: the faster I wanted to get home to examine the pamphlet, the longer it seemed to take my legs to cover the distance. I held on to my briefcase with a mixture of anticipation and trepidation, as if I had found it to be full of stolen cash. I was relieved that no-one had opened the envelope before I had a chance to. The mixture of revulsion and fascination that I had felt on seeing the Triple Cross would not be unique to me; but it was not to be shared. And there were those names, my baptismal first name as well as my surname, on the table of contents. For the first time in many years I recalled a decision I had not taken lightly. It hadn't been for any trivial reason that, years ago, I had made it clear that I wished to be known as Alin rather than Alexandru.

Once in the lift I glanced at the letters I'd taken from my mailbox in the lobby. There was one with American stamps with a Chicago postmark, and my address written in the same handwriting as the padded envelope. The lift halted at my floor; I started when the door opened, like a child discovered doing something it shouldn't, but there was no-one there waiting to get into the lift with me. I locked the door of my apartment behind me and sat down and sliced open the new envelope.

There was a single sheet of paper, with a few typewritten sentences.

> You will have received *The Martyr*. It is extremely rare and doubtless very valuable: be careful with it. Only one edition was published, before it was banned and destroyed by the false friend Antonescu. One who escaped and survived has guarded the memory and legacy of *The Martyr*. Everything for the Nation! What did your father tell you, Alexandru? What are you going to do? Where do you stand?

There was no address or signature. Nevertheless I was beginning to piece things together. But before I went any further I needed a shower and a drink. A few minutes later, with my hair still damp and a bottle of dark beer in my hand, I padded into the living room and saw the envelopes still there on the table. It was still all real, after all. In Oradea I had bought a new recording of Bach's *St. Matthew Passion* on CD; I loaded the discs into the player, took a gulp of beer, and sat down to think.

My father: he was Iulian Neascu, who had been the one who insisted on naming me Alexandru after his father. I never understood why he had done that. My grandfather had been an enthusiastic member of the Iron Guard, who had left his wife behind in Steaua de Munte when he took his son—my father—with him to Bucharest, when my grandmother had not proved to be a suitable wife for him. It was my father who had told me what little I knew about my grandfather: that he was a journalist and writer who

106

had begun to make something of a name for himself, before being taken up in the Legionary scene of Bucharest; he was a Romanian who had been able to make use of the numerous opportunities presented when Jewish writers and journalists were dismissed or not allowed to publish their work. There had been a couple of plays, and a book of short stories. But he had vanished in 1941 during the aftermath of the attempted coup against the dictator Ion Antonescu. I never knew if he'd played an active part in the revolt that had sealed the fate of the fledgling National Legionary State, but he had never been seen again in Bucharest—or anywhere else. Friends had ensured that my father was able to get back safely to Steaua de Munte, where he lived under the shadow of having had a father who was a Legionary—not that there weren't many who did not have some measure of that dark and bloody heritage. My grandfather's work disappeared from sight. My father had not inherited any magazines, books, or manuscripts; and so neither had I. My father had died just before Romania joined the European Union. He had been well into his eighties, a greatly respected man in his home town. All my friends commiserated with me after his death, but it had all left me cold. I had disowned him. My father had named me Alexandru after his own fascist father; and as far as I was concerned, that had made him as good as a fascist himself.

I read the letter again. *What did your father tell you, Alexandru? What are you going to do? Where do you stand?* As far as I knew my father hadn't really told me anything, just a bare outline. That was the trouble. If he had disagreed with his father's views, why hadn't he said so? I had no doubt that it was true that my father had suffered for being the son of Alexandru Neascu; but he had never condemned the older man and had even perpetuated his name. That is what I had never been able to understand. And my father would never explain. So I had come to feel that he must have shared my grandfather's fascism. And in the absence of evidence to the contrary I had left it at that. I altered my name and built myself a life in the same town as my father. It was the same home town to at least three generations of the Neascu men. No-one—and particularly not a member of my own family, whatever I felt about him—was going to deny me my roots in the town of my birth.

Then I carefully opened *The Martyr* again and started to read it from the beginning, except for my grandfather's piece, which I decided to leave until last. Before long I found that I was skimming over entire paragraphs and stanzas—I couldn't force myself to read every word. The stories and poems were appalling, and not only because of their subject. The poems were mainly anaemic yet overheated hymns to Corneliu Zelea Codreanu, "the Captain" and founder of the Iron Guard. The authors praised death, courted it, longed for it, boasted of giving it to others; reading sentiments like those in the grey and crumbling pages of such a shoddily-printed pamphlet was almost funny. I read through the stories, and they were much the same, except without the straining efforts made by the writers of verse to achieve rhyme. Everything was expressed in the most stale terms, with no cliché left unused and with no crime too great to be committed if the end—as decreed by Codreanu—justified the means. The Romania of *The Martyr* wasn't my country, the admittedly flawed one I recognised. Instead, it was a nightmarish mixture of farm and concentration camp, presided over by allegedly rational human beings who were more like the celebrants of a perverted church liturgy performed in a slaughterhouse. The foundations of that state were shifting and the emptiness within growing as the voices became louder and more insistent.

After my first contact with *The Martyr* I needed to feel clean water washing over me. In the shower I wished that the water would flow through my head and clean my mind, and not just my body. Afterwards I opened another bottle of beer. The Bach still playing in the background seemed more appropriate than ever. Then I decided that I must still look at Alexandru Neascu's story, whatever it turned out to be like. I settled back down again and started to read "The Windowless Room". When I had finished I got up and walked around the room. It was beginning to get dark outside, and I opened the balcony doors to let in more of the cool air of twilight.

The story was short. It had that merit at least. And it was different to all the others that I had read in *The Martyr*. I'm not a great reader and make no pretence to having any knowledge of literature or the ability to criticise it. But it seemed to me that while the other stories were set squarely in the time they were written, and tried to reflect the situation of the country as the authors saw it—from the viewpoint of the Iron Guard, and conforming to its ideology—there was no attempt in my grandfather's story to do that. Or rather, not to do so in the same way. The windowless room with its design and contents, together with the house, were clearly supposed to be fantastic and symbolic. I recognised the obvious: that the "Movement" he wrote about was the Legion; everything else was a re-hashed summary of the view my grandfather had of recent history, surrounded by old-fashioned literary absurdities such as naming the town S—— instead of using a real name or creating a credible fictional alternative.

Even though I had taken two showers, after finishing reading *The Martyr* I still felt soiled. My hands were indeed grubby, covered with dust and ink from handling the booklet, and I felt polluted in my mind as well. I had allowed it to be invaded. I shook my head as if that could loosen the black and poisonous seeds now lodged inside. And the worst thing of all was that it was a member of my own family who had infected me. I tucked the pamphlet and letter back into the padded envelope and put it away in one of the low cupboards beneath the window. I drank another bottle of beer and ate some cold pizza left over from the night before. The *St. Matthew Passion* came to its discordant end, and there was nothing left but to go to bed and attempt to leave further thinking behind me for the night.

On Saturdays when I was at home I usually opened all the windows and doors in the apartment, even in winter, and let the breeze blow away the previous week. I ate fresh warm rolls for breakfast and made a pot of my best gourmet coffee while my apartment breathed fresh and clean air—as I did too.

In fine weather I usually spent the morning wandering around Steaua de Munte, looking in antique shops in the Old Town and along the boulevards, or climbing to the top of one of the hills to enjoy the view over the huddled red roofs below to the mountains in the distance. In the warm breeze and bright sunshine of the morning I felt clean and renewed. The grim fanatical world of *The Martyr* was another place, back in the darkness where it belonged. I walked along King Carol I Boulevard and crossed the river into the New Town. That area had always been my favourite part of Steaua de Munte: I valued its regular grid of streets and squares, with their orderliness and intimacy, and the way its architecture effortlessly combined everyday humane and urbane values and proportions with touches of the baroque and strange.

I sat down on a bench under an empty pedestal in the centre of Bruckenthal Square. Presumably there had been a statue there once, but I'd never been able to find out of whom it had been. Bruckenthal Square lay on the outskirts of the New Town. When it was planned and built it had been at the edge of the countryside; but now the fields had long been covered with a district of small factories, shops, and apartment blocks that had followed in the wake of the coming of the railway. Now the whole area was waiting for the tide of restoration to reach and flow over it. The houses in the next street towards the river—nearer to the walls surrounding the Old Town—had already been restored. Their walls were painted in pastel shades of yellow and gold, green, and blue, with windows and corners picked out in white. They presented a great contrast to the houses lining the square, only a few metres away but several decades behind. The colours there were dirty and dull, with paint peeling from the buildings and stucco often crumbling away to expose the brickwork beneath. Most of the houses seemed to be empty, the paint worn off their wooden doors and shutters and their vacant windows staring blearily out over uneven pavements. And yet this was one of my favourite parts of Steaua de Munte. I enjoyed its untidy bareness as a corrective to the quiet beauty of the rest of the New Town. I knew that it couldn't remain like that for much longer.

As I sat in the sun, my gaze wandered along the row of houses opposite. In the centre of the row was a slightly larger house with a shallow porch surmounted by a large round-headed window. There was also an archway on the left leading to a courtyard at the back. Although I had sat in the square many times—too many to count—for as long as I could remember, this time a vague thought fluttered at the back of my mind. I started to get up, but just then the bell of the church on the corner of the square started to strike the hour. I hesitated and sat back down again. I looked up at the tower. It was covered in scaffolding; a Lutheran church whose restoration was being paid for by Lutherans living in Germany, some of them possibly distant relatives and descendants of those for whom it had been built. The church and tower were a smoke-dulled yellow and white. And I remembered.

I caught a tram part of the way home, and then took a shortcut through the centre of the Old Town, past the arched cemetery gate at the bottom of Star Hill. *What did your father tell you, Alexandru? What are you going to do? Where do you stand?* I was already sure that my father had told me nothing of any significance; but that also meant that I had no responsibility for doing anything or for taking a stand. What am I going to do? Carry on as usual. I'm content with my life. Where do I stand? Where I am, as Alin Neascu, a self-made man sometimes tempted to think about worshipping his creator, but in reality not that stupid. Yet as I sat at my desk and switched on the computer, things did seem different. The journey back home had not taken very long, but it had been long enough. What am I going to do? Try to find out about my grandfather and father and the Iron Guard connection once and for all. Where do I stand? No idea. And I didn't like that feeling very much.

I'm used to searching the internet, but surprises still appear. The most innocuous search terms and combinations of words can bring up the most unexpected results. I had no idea that there were so many websites and online forums dedicated to the Iron Guard. Apart from the online encyclopaedias, there were numerous sites created by academics and students. Out of those, the sites I explored looked genuinely scholarly and produced for educational and research purposes. They attempted to distinguish between what could be thought of as the less negative aspects of the Iron Guard—its pledge to end corruption and exploitation, for example—and its own unique concoction of nationalism, religious mysticism, and spectacularly brutal anti-Semitism. But there were also many sites out there in cyberspace because their creators believed in the Legion and its aims. Those online forums I could view without creating an account and logging in were highly repulsive at best. Victimhood and perceived victimhood knew no bounds, and could only be assuaged by creating new victims. And not all the sites seemed to have been created by Romanians.

Eventually I found a website that mentioned *The Martyr*, but only to comment on its rarity and describe its legendary status amongst old Legionaries. I followed links, and ended up on a webpage that listed Iron Guard "nests" that had once existed in various towns in Romania. By the time I clicked on the link to Steaua de Munte, it was with a weary resignation to the inevitable.

It turned out that Steaua de Munte, like nearly all towns of any size in Romania, possessed its own "Green House"—the headquarters of the local Iron Guard, modelled on the main one in Bucharest. Unlike the buildings built by the totalitarian parties in Germany, Italy, and the Soviet Union, the Iron Guard's buildings were nearly always extremely modest. They were often ordinary houses converted to their new purpose. Some looked like attractive residences in respectable suburbs; others were apartments, rented rooms, or small meeting halls. The website showed a contemporary postcard of the Green House in Steaua de Munte. It was the house in Bruckenthal Square.

❧

Now I had to start putting things together. The past was backing-up and beginning to stream into my life like cold and bitter water breaking through barriers and devastating the clean land on the other side. It felt as if my grandfather and father were breaking into my world, the world I had carefully created and maintained as best I could, free and safe from fanaticisms and nationalisms—in fact, from all ideologies. I liked that world. I wanted to preserve it, even from my own family. But I knew one thing for certain. One way or another, I was going to get inside the house in Bruckenthal Square and see for myself. I detest living under illusions, or having other people's delusions forced on me. That was another thing I disliked in my grandfather and my father: they had lived under delusions, and done nothing about it; my grandfather, at least, had been open as he tried to promote that Iron Guard dream of a cleansed and revived nation, without caring about the cost. If my world changed, at least it would be replaced by a better, more accurate reality; and the cost to me would be entirely worth it—and harm no-one else.

The next day I wandered around my apartment, re-reading *The Martyr* and searching the internet. Eventually I had enough and I went out, walking through the Old Town and along the restored streets next to the river. I tried to avoid crossing the river and walking through the New Town, but I found myself strolling through the sunlit baroque streets. Church bells rang and couples and families promenaded along the pavements and under the trees. Restaurants and bars, many newly opened, were doing good business. I avoided Bruckenthal Square, circling the streets around it, and stopping occasionally for a beer and snack. Walking back towards the river, I saw the yellow and white tower of the church obscured by its scaffolding rising over the rooftops. Beyond I could see the bulk of Castle Hill, rearing up with its pile of white and red buildings surmounting it, bright in the late afternoon sun. The great grey-buttressed stone gothic church, the castle's chapel, perched on the cliff high over the river, its tall slim windows flashing and shining. It was seemingly frozen in place as if by some sort of benign magic, defying gravity as it clung there, always about to collapse into the water but never doing so. It symbolised the ancient and confident town where I had been born and brought up, and in which I was proud to live. At least for as long as my ancestry was not known. Then I realised that the church tower had remained in sight, and I had entered Bruckenthal Square. I walked past the house quickly, and hoped that no-one had noticed. It was as if the sunlit town had been overshadowed by a dark cloud. I hurried back to my apartment.

Early on Monday morning I woke up in a state of indecision. Unavoidably, and luckily, I had to drive to Braşov to meet clients, and then go on with them to Predeal. The travelling, the meetings and discussions, together with the necessity of having to drive back to Steaua de Munte the same evening, meant that the day passed quickly. By the time I got home, I was feeling pleasantly tired. In the lobby I unlocked my mailbox and pulled out the few envelopes waiting for me. One of them felt lumpy as I grasped it; I looked more closely and saw that it was another padded envelope bearing American stamps with a Chicago postmark. The handwriting was by now very familiar. I controlled myself enough not to tear open the envelope there and then, in view of the receptionist and some of my neighbours. In the lift I shook the envelope, but the lumps merely redistributed themselves. Perhaps they were old coins or medals.

In my apartment I ripped open the envelope and shook it out over the table. There was no letter or other enclosure, but two long keys fell out and clattered onto the polished wooden surface. I didn't need to ask which doors they were made to open. I examined the keys closely. One seemed to be an ordinary, heavy key suitable for an ordinary, heavy front door. It radiated security and respectability, suitable for a fine house in a good square in the New Town. The other key was much more modern. It seemed to fly up into my hand, meeting it half-way as I reached for it. It fitted into my grasp and I took hold of it. Then I almost flung the key at the open window in surprise, as it generated an odd and disconcerting feeling, swiftly followed by revulsion. It was like picking up a small coin and feeling it move because it was really a spider. As I took another look at the key close up I saw that the bow was cut into the design of the Iron Guard's Triple Cross.

Moonlight flooded through the great round-headed window, bathing the hall and staircase with wan light. I trod lightly past the bottom of the stairs. The hall was clean and there was very little dust; I assumed that the house was maintained, cleaned regularly. I didn't know how far back the house extended from the street. No doubt there was a garden as well as the courtyard, so perhaps there was a wing or back extension that would have allowed for the building of the windowless room that my grandfather described. Unless that part of the story was fiction. But somehow I thought not; it would not have been in character. I crept through an open archway to the right of the stairs. It opened onto a long corridor, a black tunnel with apparently no windows to allow in even the merest glimmer of light. I switched on my torch and advanced further into the corridor. On the left I made out several doorways, at evenly-spaced intervals. As I passed each one, I knocked on the door and opened it. I don't know how I would have reacted if there had been an answer to my knock or if the door had been pulled from inside as I pushed it open.

The corridor seemed longer than it was possible for it to be, judging from what I had been able to survey of the exterior of the house. As I measured off paces I thought that if I'd been outside I would have reached the next street by now. I knocked on the fourth door. Immediately I could tell that there was an inconsistency. Even though my knuckles touched the door only for a second, it still felt distinctly different to the others. Also the noise that my knocking made was not the same as for the other doors. The sound was muffled; there was certainly a room behind the door, but it was as if the very air in the room was at variance to what it should be. There was a new resonance. I tried to open the door. Unlike the others, it did not open when I pushed it. I stepped back from the door and pulled the second key out of my pocket. I felt the Triple Cross design against my palm as I grasped the key. Again it seemed to fit into my hand, ease its way into the contours of my palm, like oil oozing into every line and crease of skin. Now that I held the key, it seemed to pull itself towards the lock, dragging my hand along with it, as if attracted by a strong magnet. Some time must have passed as I stood in the black corridor; fractions of a second, or hours, I couldn't tell. The door opened slowly, and I glided forward and entered the room.

The door closed behind me. The walls and floor of the windowless room glowed with an inner radiance. I remembered my grandfather's story. The room was a cube. Now the lamps on the centre of each wall started to glow dully, and I could see more of the room. In the exact centre stood an ebony table; there was a box resting on it. I found myself standing next to the table. I reached out for the box and felt the raised Triple Cross design of the lid as my palm pressed itself against it. The box had no lock, but now one wasn't necessary. I couldn't force myself to look down at the floor, not immediately. And then I knew I wasn't alone.

There was a sense of dread, and then vertigo, as if I were looking down a deep well. It was all too easy to imagine the foulness and slime at the bottom, with the fetor drifting up into the clean daylight at ground level and polluting it. My feet grew cold, and the sense of dread increased. I could not move. The mood of anxiety I was experiencing was as nothing to that which I felt coming from the—other—in the windowless room. And yet I knew I was being welcomed.

The Windowless Room of Iulian Neascu

Now that I am about to become a father, I owe it to myself and to my unborn son—for I know he will be a son—to explain my thoughts and actions to him. And how can I explain? During the turbulent years when I was growing up, I was so proud of my own father. I grew to adulthood during the reign of King Carol II and the endless shuffling of Prime Ministers and Cabinets that he presided over. My father, with his poems, stories, plays, and essays, was always a constant challenge and irritant to the current regime. He saw through the tawdriness and the empty glory of the public spectacles. He saw through to the essential country, his beloved Romania that lay beneath them. He ridiculed and pilloried those who boasted that they wanted everything for the nation and nothing against the nation, while at the same time undermining it.

My teenage years coincided with the rise of the Iron Guard. My father was one of their chief targets, and I was caught up too. At school I endured taunting and being ostracised. I learned to defend myself with my fists as well as standing up for myself with what I could say. Because of all this I had few friends. The certainty of returning home each day to a family whose ideals I loved was all that gave me any real purpose. And then my father joined the Iron Guard.

His defection was celebrated. I was congratulated for his repentance. But my mother and I were devastated. When my father moved to Bucharest to put his skills at the service of Codreanu's thugs I went with him only because my mother begged me to. She did not want me to share her humiliation in Steaua de Munte. But once in the capital I found a place of my own to live and my own small circle of friends. Nevertheless my father's surname tainted my own, and that was unavoidable. I was always aware that my father's name was also my own, and that was unavoidable. It soon began to dawn on me that I owed a greater loyalty to the family, as represented by its name. Our family existed before the Monarchy and regime. There was no reason why it should not outlast them. It could even outlast the country. Lines on maps and areas of land ruled over by leaders and governments can change, but there are always people. In a way that I cared for not at all, it also meant that I still owed loyalty to my father. Without him I could not have come to be. I had to set that aside even as I hated his decision to place himself and all his talents at the service of a group of gangsters. And, of course, I still harboured terrible thoughts about what I would have done if I had been in his place. I could not then answer that question. I still cannot. And so I cannot entirely reject my father, much as I might wish to. We are all caught in a giant web. The Iron Guard was led by a ghost. The dead led the living, and everyone was marching into the grave. They proclaimed the brotherhood of all Romanians—the dead, the living, and the souls of the unborn. So we are all damned.

The past is inescapable, for it is all there is. To this day I do not know what happened to my father. I do not truly know whether or not I ought to be loyal to the living or the dead. But I am, because I cannot help it and I must. We remain in uneasy, and for me unwanted, communion. And now I know more, perhaps all. It is said that to know all is to forgive all. That is too simple, too much of a sweeping statement. There are enough of those. I cannot forgive, as much as I might understand. Now I am in a hell because I know all. I cannot bear to pass this information on to my son.

I hoped that my inner migration has been a subtle enough one. Perhaps it will prove to have been too subtle. I conform outwardly. But then, so does almost everyone. Surely that is acceptable? Family loyalty demands ignorance as well as knowledge, the blessing of obscuring darkness as well as the cleansing and healing light. Perhaps my son will find out for himself. In any case, I know how I must act. No light enters or escapes from the windowless room. Neither does the darkness grow, nor can it escape. The Form remains in its state of being and not-being, simultaneously. All the possibilities of the nation remain to coalesce into certainty. I am an inevitable part of it, but will always remain at the centre, held in hard iron darkness and chill marble.

❧

At home once more, I put the ragged copy of *The Martyr*, the letter, and the keys on the table and sat down, staring at them. I began to consider what had I felt and possibly even seen, as the lamps had flared up briefly before dimming back down into darkness once more. In the house the moonlight shone and the bells marked the hours. I had got out of the windowless room, but I was sure that I had left something of myself behind. After all, we are still family. Time and space scarcely matter, scarcely count for anything.

So much of what I had thought I knew was wrong. I had given loathing instead of sympathy, betrayal instead of loyalty—and without cause, unlike my father to his father. Maybe we all need to experience a hell of some sort. I wondered if my grandfather's conversion to the Iron Guard and its ideology had been his escape, even as he condemned his wife and son to their anguish. Perhaps my grandfather's hell was a deeper dissembling of a sort that my father's was nothing by comparison. Or perhaps my grandfather did die in the bloody chaos of the early 1940s, and the way of his death had been torment enough. And the windowless room consumed both my father and grandfather. Maybe my hell was going to be one of mere knowledge: inaction and the inability to take any action, because other forces were too strong and I couldn't get the better of them. And there remained the three questions.

The memories came flooding back. It was my sixteenth birthday. My father took me to Bucharest as a special treat. It was supposed to be a surprise, but my parents had dropped hints about it for weeks beforehand. And I had gone along with it all. My father fixed things so we could eat a lavish meal in a restaurant close to the Calea Victoriei. We went to a large bookshop near the university, and he bought me a beautifully illustrated book on Byzantine ikons that I had seen in the university library in Steaua de Munte, and had been longing for. It had been published abroad and must have cost my father a fortune in import charges and other costs. Then we walked to the Athenaeum, where my father wanted to show me the mosaics and frescoes, and had booked seats for a concert. When we got there I stood under the portico and refused point-blank to accompany my father inside. I remembered that I'd told him that I detested his fascism and how he hid it by outward conformity to the People's Republic. I said that if I could vomit up the meal I would, and I didn't want to be seen with him anymore in Bucharest, and certainly not in the Athenaeum. I held out my hand for my train ticket, so I could travel home immediately. My father said nothing while I was telling him the home truths that I had carefully nurtured. He winced as I demanded my ticket, and turned away and wiped his eyes, pretending some dust had got into them. He handed our concert tickets to a young couple who had been hesitantly looking at a poster, whispering about the prices. Then without a word my father tried to take my arm; he smiled shyly and hopefully, as if he were about to say something. I shook him off. We walked back to the station in silence. I had thrown my father's love and pride in his growing son back into his face, I had taken pleasure in doing so. And I had always felt proud of myself for doing that.

My eyes were smarting with tears as I pulled a suitcase out from the bottom of a cupboard. The book was still there: the beautiful book on ikons that I had kept, even though if I'd really been true to my convictions I would have thrown it into the Dâmbovița during my birthday outing. I had kept the book not because I wanted to spare something of my father's feelings, but because I was selfish and wanted to possess it. And I cried as I slowly turned the pages and the gazed at the parade of solemn faces; the sad, all-knowing eyes of the various Christs and all his saints bored into my soul. Later I sent an email to one of the partners saying that a family emergency had occurred, and that I would very likely not be able to come into the office for a few days.

Early the next morning I drove across the mountains to Bucharest. I parked my car close to the Athenaeum, and walked down the Calea Victoriei towards the Dâmboviţa. I held an envelope containing a few thousand lei, which I was going to throw into the river. I crossed Lipscani Street and passed the Stavropoleos Church. I realised that my intended sacrifice could be made useful. I entered the tall dim church, with its smoke-darkened paintings and glowing islands of candles. I thrust the envelope into the hands of the first nun I saw, and rushed back out into the daylight before she could say anything or ask any questions. On my way back to the Athenaeum it started to pour with rain; the thunderstorm seemed to be directly over the canyon-like street, and I started to get wet. I began to cry. I stumbled along, wiping my face so the rain hid my tears. By the time I reached my car I was thoroughly drenched. People sought shelter from the downpour under the portico of the Athenaeum. I walked past them towards my car, taking off my jacket as I approached it. I thought I heard murmuring, maybe the people sheltering from the rain were discussing this drunkard who was doing nothing to stop himself from getting wet. When I was in range I aimed the key and opened the doors of my car, and made the roof open as well. Then I sat in the driver's seat as the torrential rain fell into my beloved car. I sat there without moving, still crying and sobbing even after the rain stopped and the sun came out again. I shivered as my soaked clothes and the interior of my car began to dry slowly. Everything would be damaged and cost me a lot to repair or replace. I sat there ignoring bystanders talking and whispering about me. For once in my life I did penance, wretched though it was. An expensive car and suit of clothes compared to a life? Nevertheless it was a start. When it looked as if I were going to attract the attention of a policeman, I drove away slowly and carefully, out of Bucharest and back to Steaua de Munte.

I call myself Alin Alexandru Neascu now. I destroyed the copy of *The Martyr* and the letter; the keys I posted back in the envelope they had arrived in, having first obliterated my name and address. I've never forgotten the three questions the letter asked. But perhaps now I have understood and even answered them, or at least started to make progress towards doing so, and a new maturity. And I have never forgotten what I thought I saw on the floor of the windowless room. It seems that the house in Bruckenthal Square remains unchanged, and I am sure that I will be better prepared if I ever receive another message from my anonymous correspondent. I only hope there will be something left of me.

To Hope for a Caesar

No bitterness: our ancestors did it,
They were only ignorant and hopeful, they wanted freedom
*   but wealth too,*
Their children will learn to hope for a Caesar.

*   – Robinson Jeffers, "Ave Caesar"*

My encounter with Matthias Bratke took place during a love affair. After a couple of years I was still as much in love with that great city, Berlin, as I ever had been. Like my home city, London, Berlin as a whole isn't a beautiful place. It can be remarkably charmless. But parts of it are quite pretty, and much of it is attractive. And certain small areas are actually stunning. I once taunted Markus, who is a Berliner born and bred, with these thoughts. But he claimed not to understand a word of what I was on about. And that's from someone who earned a PhD for researching and writing a thesis on the International Style in Berlin.

Markus claims never to quite understand my infatuation with his native city. But it helps to pay our bills, so he is happy to go along with it. There are no well-paying jobs in Berlin for people with doctorates in architecture, so he works in a library on one of the outer housing estates in the former East, and is grateful for it. So as well as my main job as a translator of technical and training manuals from English into German—in fact anything that needs translating, I will have a go at it—I also spend most of my free time, especially in the tourist season, taking small groups of tourists on guided tours around the city. I offer several variations, from the basic, which includes all of the expected locations—the Reichstag building, Brandenburg Gate, Unter den Linden, Television Tower, and so on—to the very specialist, like for instance my Weimar Republic Art Deco Architecture tour, or my traces of the German Democratic Republic tour. (Markus is from the former East—he gave me a lot of tips for that one.)

This particular time I was conducting quite a general tour. Five people had signed up. There were two young-ish couples: one American and one English, plus an older, almost elderly, lone man, German himself from what few words he had spoken so far. He had been giving me the creeps somewhat. I felt as if I should've known him, and he knew that—which gave him an advantage over me that he would know how to make use of.

On this particular afternoon in May, we were standing in the Wilhelmstrasse. It was near the end of the tour. This had been one of the middle-ranking tours, neither slumming it entirely for the tourists, nor so specialised that I had to carry notes or even a laptop with me. It was the Government Quarter Old and New tour: Reichstag, the new Federal Government buildings along the River Spree, the new and restored embassy buildings, plus the sites of buildings that once housed people who changed the course of history, and who wiped millions out of their way, before they were themselves eradicated.

The Wilhelmstrasse is nothing special to look at now. Most of the street is occupied by blocks of flats, the system-built apartments of the Communist era. Admittedly they are the upmarket ones. Hardly anything is left of the street from where Bismarck and Hitler conducted their foreign policies and much more. There is little else but the gigantic survival of the building constructed to house Hermann Göring's Air Ministry. (I like to tell people that it's so big because it was built to allow planes to land on its roof. I've never discovered whether that was actually true or not, but I like the thought, and it usually raises a laugh.) It was nearly the end of the tour. We had walked, for ever it seemed, along the pavement in front of the former Air Ministry building. Now we were sheltering from the sun under the covered entrance at the south end of the building.

"It's now used by the Federal Finance Ministry," I said. "All the eagles and swastikas were knocked off almost immediately after the war ended. There was a directive issued to all local authorities to remove all objectionable symbols. The German Democratic Republic was proclaimed from in there, and the Berlin Wall ran right next to it, just around the corner." I pointed to a short stretch of battered, graffiti-covered concrete wall. "There isn't much more than that left in the entire city," I said.

"Isn't Checkpoint Charlie close by?" the American woman asked.

"Yes, it is, just over there, along the Zimmerstrasse." I pointed in the other direction across the street. "This tour ends here, in a few minutes, but you can get to Checkpoint Charlie on your own easily enough."

I didn't quite say that I don't do Disneyland.

"Now that you're here look around you, use your imaginations," I said. "Imagine what it would've been like in this street in May 1945. One of the world's most important streets, full of rubble and bordered by ruins. Imagine Whitehall or Pennsylvania Avenue like that. What the impact was." I returned to an earlier theme in the tour. "There was a time of total devastation, both physical and moral. Berliners called it Zero Hour. When the guns stopped firing and the bombs had finally stopped falling, and the rebuilding could begin."

The American woman clapped politely. I smiled and laughed. I didn't pass the hat around—I already had their cheques or cash in my pocket. But I have sometimes been tipped. Every little helps . . .

"I hope you all enjoyed the tour and thought it was worthwhile." I handed out some flyers. "Here is a selection of some of the other tours that I do. Of course, I can lay on something special if you like. Please just get in touch. Tell your friends." I nodded around at everyone in general, and began to back away slightly, so that I could make a quick escape. I wanted to meet Markus at the Potsdamer Platz.

The English couple thanked me and walked back the way we had just come. The Americans seemed to be hesitating about whether to go to Checkpoint Charlie or not. The elderly man just stood there, looking at the fragment of the Wall as if he'd never seen it before. I put my spare flyers away, and was just about to walk off along the Niederkirchnerstrasse, the quickest way to Potsdamer Platz. I made the mistake of glancing at him again. He had close-cropped white hair and beard. A smile, almost a smirk, played around his lips, then disappeared. He looked as if he were trying to summon up the nerve to speak, or was weighing up what nerve I would need to make the appropriate response to what he wanted to say.

"My young man, you speak German very well," he said.

I recalled that near the beginning of the tour I'd got rid of some over-enthusiastic street-vendors.

"Thank you. It didn't come easily."

He smiled again, and shook his head. "I can only imagine. Still, you know what we say: 'German language, difficult language'."

For some reason I found myself not wanting to rush away so quickly. "Yes, that's true, it is. For me, learning German was like getting punched in the face, and then receiving a big sloppy kiss from the one who'd hit me. I loved every minute of it!"

Then I knew that I had said too much and had been far too open with him. I glanced at my watch.

"You are in a hurry? You see, I think you will be able to help me."

I thought that maybe he was going to ask me to have a drink or even a meal with him, or worse. It had happened before. In a way it was flattering. To some people I seem to represent a certain something, I've never quite worked out what. But then I realised he just wanted to speak to me. Okay, I could put up with that. He may be able to recommend me to others. Maybe he had some piece of first-hand local history or knowledge to pass on.

"No, I've got a few minutes. Do you want to find somewhere to sit down?"

"No, it is all right. I will not take up much of your valuable time. But I do think you will be able to help me."

The situation was becoming like pure John le Carré. The American couple had walked away. No-one else was in earshot.

"So what can I do for you, sir?"

"I need to you to contact someone for me. I know he is in Berlin. He is a German, yet his English is excellent, almost that of a native speaker. I need him to meet with me, but I do not quite wish to approach him so directly. He will listen to someone like you. You are—you are young, neutral."

I laughed. I couldn't help it. "We need to be at Checkpoint Charlie," I said. "Or at the Glienicke Bridge. This does seem so very Cold War!"

The smile froze on his face. "Do not laugh, please. I am serious. I need to speak to a certain man before it is too late, and I am sure that you can help me in this. It is more important than you seem to realise."

"I apologise, sir. Please forgive me. They say anything can happen in Berlin—"

He gave a sudden, fast, almost military nod. "They are right," he snapped. "Now please. I have observed you at work. You are diligent, thoughtful. You know your history, your Berlin. Well, so do I. I know too much of it too well. Now, there is a man who has recently started to drink his coffee at the same café that you do. He is a very distinguished looking man—"

I was sure I knew who he was talking about—by sight, anyway. He was solidly built—not stout or fat, but certainly substantial. Probably all muscle. I'd wondered about him. I'd thought that he could either be a hit-man or a priest. In the small café, he walked easily, almost nonchalantly, carrying his weight lightly. He'd looked down at me once, when I was working at a translation and a large slice of coffee cake. He hadn't smiled, but he'd raised his eyebrows and his blue eyes had twinkled wickedly. He'd made me feel good. Simply that. But something had also made me feel that he did not carry that gift as easily as his body. When I had told Markus about it, he'd said that he thought he'd noticed him as well, strolling around an exhibition at the New National Gallery. It was almost certainly the same man. "Probably everyone in Berlin has now seen him," Markus had said.

"Yes, I've seen him. He's a German? I'd always thought that he must be an expatriate Englishman."

"No, he is a German. Sort of, but true German enough. Actually he and his ancestry is what they mistakenly still call Saxon. He comes from the Siebenbürgen—you would know that, I think, as Transylvania. He comes from a country of small, walled towns surrounded by people who disliked for centuries the inhabitants who dwelt within them. But in any event, he is a special man. Now, as you have seen him, you will know what I mean when I say that . . . "

I nodded.

"I require to meet with him. More than that, I would really not like to say to you now. Please tell him next time you see him. Give him my card." He handed me a small white sealed envelope. "I think that he will meet with me. I would like you to be there too, when we meet."

Now it was the old man's turn to look at his watch.

"It is I who must go," he said. He held out his hand. "My young man, I thank you. I will see you again soon, I feel sure."

I shook his hand. The grip was much stronger than I had been expecting. Suddenly I felt like I was back at school, when I met the headmaster in his study for the first time.

"But . . . Whom shall I say . . . ? And what's . . . ?"

"Oh yes. My name is Althaus. Tell him that—Theodor Althaus. And our friend's name—it is Mr. Matthias Bratke. Until later, then. Good day, my dear young man."

❧

Markus was on his second beer when I got to the bar.

"Steve, you are late, did you drag your clients all the way out to Tempelhof Airport again, or did you get taken somewhere?"

He grinned.

"I earned us mucho euro," I said. "Let's have a couple of those."

Eventually I started to tell Markus about what had happened.

"Mr. Althaus? He said his name is Althaus? That sounds like a false name to me, but a more interesting choice than some of the German surnames that he thought an educated Englishman like you might know. At least he did not call himself Mr. Schmidt or Mr. Schumacher! Are you going to go along with this?"

"Yes."

"Steve, you do worry me sometimes. You do not know what you are getting into, what you might be getting us both into."

"You said that you'd seen Bratke. I think if you'd been asked to talk to him you would've done as well. Am I right, Markus?"

"Maybe. Maybe not. Berlin has blinded you, Steve."

I finished my beer.

"No, you're the one that's blinded me. And I love it. Berlin's the backdrop. But what a backdrop. This couldn't happen in any other city in the world, I know it."

❧

The next morning Markus still looked at me as if I were a bit mad, as if I were some foreigner with an infatuation, who needed to be protected a little until it wore off. But I had been through that stage, and had come out the other side. Markus went to work, and I packed up my laptop and headed out. The sealed envelope was in my pocket.

I had no tours scheduled that day or the next. I sat in the café, drinking coffee after coffee, and holding out more or less successfully against the temptations of the cakes that Jens, the owner, kept putting in my way. I worked on a rough translation of an article on Albert Speer's plans for Berlin. At least that was interesting, but even so my mind wasn't really on it. I knew that I'd have to check it over very carefully indeed. I kept looking up to see if Bratke had come in. But there was no sign of him. After a few hours I packed up and went home.

The next day I returned to the café and continued to work and look. Normally I would also have to think about going around tourist areas like Zoo Station or the Brandenburg Gate and hand out flyers, trying to drum-up tour business. But I didn't want to risk missing Bratke.

After a couple of hours he came in. He sat down at the table next to mine. I wanted to catch his eye, but I didn't want to make him think that I was after him for anything. Even though I was. Jens brought Bratke a coffee, and I signalled for another one as well. Bratke sipped at his coffee, and then looked straight at me. We were sitting only about three feet apart.

"So, what do you want to say?"

I almost shoved my laptop off the table. "Pardon?"

"I've seen you in here before. I think that, like me, you've come to treat this place as your local coffee house? As your watching-post in Berlin? I've seen you in here with your partner. He is your partner, isn't he?"

I nodded.

"Okay. Listen, I've got something of a reputation for being wired-in when it comes to people. I can tell that you have something to say to me. A question, perhaps?" He sipped more coffee. "Or a request? Come on now, out with it. I've asked enough questions!"

I had put Althaus's envelope on the table next to my laptop. Maybe I'd been glancing at it a lot. I picked it up and held it out to Bratke. He smiled. I immediately felt more at ease.

"Ah, I wondered if that might be relevant. But first, let's introduce ourselves. My name is Bratke, Matthias Anton

Bratke. You can call me Matthias or Mr. Bratke. Whichever. And you are Stephen McDowell, and you probably know this city much better than I do."

I pointed at the envelope.

"I prefer being called Steve. Anyway, I met this old guy, ah, a couple of days ago. He was on one of my tours. He knew about you. He wanted me to give you that envelope. I don't know what's in it."

"Hmm. No-one knows about me. But let's see."

Bratke tore the envelope open, and pulled out a small card.

"Dr. Theodor Althaus. He's using his real name, then."

I took a gulp of my coffee. I needed its heat and bitter strength right then. What was I getting in to?

"Right."

Bratke said, "You're not impressed."

"You're wrong there. I've been impressed, no, very impressed, for the last few minutes at least. You seem to know more about all this, about me, about everything, than I do."

"You've never heard of Dr. Theodor Althaus, then?"

I shook my head. "No. My—Markus thought it wasn't his real name. Should I have told him?"

Bratke smiled. "I'm sure that was all right. Two are better than one, so they say." A momentary pain showed in his eyes, a mental grimace. "It can help to share, even to have only shared in the past. But yes, Althaus is his real name, and I suppose it's not surprising that you haven't heard of him. He was very good at his chosen profession. Theodor Althaus was a high-ranking member of the old German Socialist Unity Party. There are probably a few people who'd like a long talk with him. I'm absolutely sure that he was big in the Stasi as well. But in all cases behind the scenes. Totally. Others took any credit or disgrace. And yet

Althaus doesn't seem to be making any attempt to disguise himself or hide away."

"The SED? Stasi? Bloody hell. Unless wanting to see you is the start of something—"

Bratke put the card down and reached over and took my hand. His own hand was warm and surprisingly soft. But I had no doubt it could've crushed mine.

"Steve, this certainly is the start of something. I felt it when I arrived in Berlin. Something was going to happen. I only had to wait. Something would happen to me or someone would trigger something. This is it. I will indeed get in touch with Dr. Theodor Althaus. And will you come with me? Steve?"

I felt Bratke's magnetism, a touch of the power that somehow came from within him. I felt that this man could've ruled an entire country if he'd put his mind to it. Yet he didn't want to manipulate. His power—that was the only word I could think of just then—created space and ease. He let go of my hand, and picked up his coffee cup. As he took a sip, he winked at me, conspiratorially. Just as with Althaus, part of it with Bratke was like meeting the headmaster, but then to have him wink at me . . . I was sold. I remembered snatches of a poem by Kurt Tucholsky about Berlin that I'd once translated as an exercise. Something like: "You spend your whole life long on a thousand streets . . . The twinkling of an eye, the calling of a soul . . . A stranger's eyes, a quick glance . . . A chance never to be repeated . . . "

"He said that he hoped to see me again as well," I said. I remembered one of Markus's favourite sayings. "What the hell. Anything should be able to happen in Berlin. I'm in!"

Bratke stood up. "Well then, that's settled. I'll make a start. How about meeting here again, this time tomorrow? Will that be okay? I will find you if things change in the meantime. Take care, Steve."

He put a few euro on the table, and strode out of the café.

Jens said, "He is a strange man, eh? Yes? And you meet him."

"Jensi, you don't know the half of it. And neither do I. See you."

I packed up my things and went out onto the street. I decided to walk home. A little research and revision was in order.

❧

At home I got onto the internet, fast. The SED: Socialist Unity Party of Germany, the result of a dubious merger between the German Communist and Social Democratic Parties, in the Soviet occupation zone, before it had become the German Democratic Republic. The Stasi: State Security Service, a legend in its own lifetime for the tenacity and ruthlessness, the quality and quantity, of its surveillance of its own people, dissidents or not. I recalled a joke that Markus told me, not long after I'd moved to Berlin. Or had it been a joke? I didn't think that Markus had been too sure either. He said that when the Stasi had been abolished, a lot of its agents got jobs as taxi drivers. They were very good. Why? You simply gave them your name, and they drove you straight to where you lived.

Online I searched for Theodor Althaus. Plenty of Althauses, any number of Theodors, but no Theodor Althaus. Not a single one. And there was not a single Matthias Bratke, either.

I was watching the early evening news when Markus got home. I poured him a glass of wine as he kicked off his boots.

"So what have you found out today?" he asked.

"Drink your wine. You look hot."

Condensation was misting on the glass, trickling down, dripping off it. I poured some wine for myself. It was sharp and cold.

Markus smiled. "That means you've got something you do want to tell me, Steve." He took a gulp of wine. "Already I'm cooling. Hey, or you're not sure about what to say."

"It's okay," I said. "Yes, I found out a bit about our Mr. Althaus. Doctor Althaus—actually and genuinely. And Althaus is his real name. I didn't like it though. Even the little bit that I found out."

For all my knowledge and enjoyment of Germany, of Berlin, I'd never found it easy to simply start talking about what happened in the past, or to ask questions about terrible events that so many older Germans would've known about, or even taken part in, one way or the other. I'd often thought that my tours were a way of getting a lot off my chest, as well as learning. No doubt the fact that most of the people who took my tours were as foreign as I was also helped. And yet, when I had got down to talking to real Berliners, often complete strangers in a bar, after many beers (all of which probably helped too) I had found no unwillingness to talk and reminisce. From people of all ages. Maybe my enthusiasm, willingness, and ability to speak reasonable German gained me goodwill. Or some of them—especially those of Althaus's age or older—were good actors and storytellers. And Markus took it all in good part.

"Althaus is not such an unusual name," Markus said.

"As was employment by the Stasi?"

"He was Stasi?"

"Bratke reckoned so. But then, just about everyone was in it, weren't they?"

"Yes, lots of people. After the Change lots of people who you think weren't anything to do with them, they had been employed by them. Like there was one of the pastors at the church near where I lived."

I shook my head. "I just about remember hearing about all that, when I was a kid. I was so interested in Germany even then! All those bastards, getting their claws into the society, into decent people, every bit of their lives. Then I read some of the stories, about the poor sods who'd informed and spied because of being blackmailed, or wanting to get their child into university, or wanting to visit someone in the West."

I drank some more wine. "I'm getting carried away. But when I think that I've actually met one of the masterminds behind it all . . . "

"Steve, you believe this Matthias Bratke, then?"

"Yeah. He seems genuine. I felt the complete opposite than how I felt when I met Althaus. And now big Matti is going to meet Dr. Althaus, and they both want me there. What am I getting into, Markus?"

He got up and went towards the kitchen. "Food is what we are getting into right now," Markus said. "Hey, just because anything can happen in Berlin, it does not mean that it has to."

As I listened to the clanging of pots and pans in the kitchen, I wondered what the hell Markus was on about. And not for the first time.

❧

I was at the café far too early the next day.

I was still in a strange mood. I'd eventually tried to talk about my new misgivings, but as I did they sounded stupid, and I'd clammed up. And I'd felt that Markus felt that they were stupid as well, or that there was something there that, for the first time between us, I was going to trespass on, and he wanted to avoid that, and knew that I'd avoid it, too, if I knew what it was. For him to say or hint more might make things worse, and uncover hidden things. But he also knew that when I got going about something, that was it, and only I could be the one who determined when my interest would be exhausted, and it was time to get back to normal.

During the time that Markus and I had been together, once or twice I had thought to myself that maybe the whole business of living in Berlin was like that—an enthusiasm that would pass. And Markus would pass with it. I didn't believe that now, but when I get thinking . . .Perhaps Markus had similar thoughts, and all the time was thinking about damage limitation. That terrified me more than meeting some old Stasi relic. It terrified me because it made me as bad as him, even if I'd never meant that to happen. But that was the oldest defence of all.

After leaving home, I'd walked past the café the first time. I saw that Jens was there, behind his counter, serving coffees and cutting his dangerous cakes into marginally less dangerous slices. All this was my world now. I'd made it my world, and it was one very different from that of my upbringing. I'd been let in to a new world, and I didn't want it to change, or to have to go back. I wandered on down the street. I had become familiar with so many of its details: the uneven road surface and the cobbles, the splashes of graffiti on some of the peeling walls, the places where the sun shone on balconies and window-boxes. I crossed the little park at the end of the street and turned off towards the Warschauer Strasse. For the first time in months I was so distracted that a tram almost ran me over. I grinned and waved at the driver and the queue at the tram-stop. If nothing else, I thought, at least I was learning to swear like a true Berliner.

Jens had just brought me my second coffee when Bratke turned up. He slipped easily into the chair opposite mine. He got straight down to business.

"Better drink that up, and we'll go and visit Theodor Althaus. I've made contact with him. He'll be expecting us."

Bratke waved Jens away apologetically as I gulped my coffee and got up.

"We'll be in later!" Bratke shouted as we went out.

"Where are we going?" I said. "Where does he live?"

"Leipziger Strasse."

I whistled. Right in the city centre, close to the main tourist hot-spots. My tours crossed and recrossed the Leipziger Strasse all the time. It would be like a Londoner living in somewhere like Kingsway or the Strand. Leipziger Strasse had been practically obliterated during the Second World War bombing, and was gradually rebuilt as a wide boulevard lined with flats. Then the street had ended squarely, solidly, at the Berlin Wall until 1989, when the city was stitched back together again. It was still rumoured that a few former German Democratic Republic officials and politicians were still living on in the upper reaches of the highest and most exclusive blocks that had been built for them. So it was certainly a fitting place for Althaus's residence.

"Bus or underground?" Bratke asked. "Which is the quickest way there?"

"Here." Scarcely even breaking our pace, we plunged down the steps into an S-Bahn station. "We'll change at Alexanderplatz, then U-Bahn to the Spittelmarkt."

"You're used to this!"

I laughed. "After London, travelling on the trains here is actually a pleasure!"

"So you already know whereabouts Dr. Althaus lives, by the look of it?"

"It can only be the Colonnade Tower, as it's called now. The most exclusive block of flats the DDR built in Berlin. You had at least to be in the Politbüro, or in line for it, to get a flat there."

We got on the train.

"Yes, you're right," Bratke said. "I got a taxi past there last night after I spoke to Althaus. That's the place, all right. And right at the top. He's got a penthouse flat."

"*The* penthouse, I expect. How did you find him to speak to?"

Bratke sighed. "He was quiet and seemed grateful that I'd done what he wanted, and gotten in touch. And he was arrogant and convinced that I'd do whatever it was that he wanted to ask of me. He made it sound like he was telling, although the words were all about asking. And he made it clear that he'd heard a lot about me."

The train lurched slightly as it drew into Alexanderplatz Station. We threaded our way through the wide passages, and up and down crowded staircases.

"He must've done, to know that I would be your go-between. It still scares me that Althaus knew that we knew each other, sort of."

"He gave me the creeps too," Bratke said, as we got onto the next train. "I mean, it wasn't just that he had heard of me, but what he knew. Steve, I've been in Germany many times, and in East Germany a few times, not always officially—"

"I'm thinking le Carré again—"

"Steve, it wasn't like that, but there were things going on you probably wouldn't believe. And that I don't think the rational Dr. Althaus would've done, either. And yet now he wants to talk, and talk to me. I had the sense that he'd been waiting for this opportunity, when I was in Berlin. I didn't know I was coming until a couple of days before I did, and yet I got the feeling that Althaus had been sitting up in his eyrie, just waiting and waiting, as if he was owed my visit. As if it would simply come to him, as of right."

"All that over the phone?"

"Yes, exactly!"

Only a few minutes later we were walking along the hot and grimy Leipziger Strasse, heading west. Behind us was the river, and fragments of the old city, ranged amongst the new like odd old teeth next to dentures. But I'd always valued that effect—and there wasn't any going back, anyway.

Colonnade Tower rose from the far side of a small square. Half of it was worn grass and dusty bushes, with a couple of tennis courts occupying the part of the square farthest away from the flats. I craned my neck looking upwards. We were standing down on the ground, in the dust and traffic, the fallen leaves and graffiti. I'd been to the supermarket in the base of the next block lots of times. But up in the tower, it was surely a different world, in time as well as space. At the entrance, Bratke pressed the button marked ALTHAUS. Without anybody saying anything, the buzzer sounded, and we walked inside. Althaus hadn't seen the need to use a different name on the street entrance, or anything like that. He certainly didn't seem to be in any sort of hiding. The lift opened out onto a white hallway, with windows on two sides. I had an overwhelming sense of sky and wind and clouds, like being on the bridge of a ship. There were two doors opposite us. The one on the right opened, and Theodor Althaus stood there.

"Come in, my gentlemen, please," he said. We shook hands as we went in. "I waited for you here myself, in case you went to the other door by an error. You see, it is still dwelt in by—" He named someone I thought had been dead for at least a decade. I thought I remembered reading his obituary, stating that he'd died in exile in Paraguay or

Uruguay or somewhere like that. "He does not see many visitors anymore, and in any case you would not wish to see him."

Althaus ushered us into his sitting room. It was sparsely but luxuriously furnished: he had been able to go for quality rather than quantity. I'd been expecting a crowded, tasteless and gilded pseudo-boudoir, the sort of place that dictators built for themselves, or that every Middle-Eastern ruler seems to have. The room was flooded with light. No-one could ever get bored with such a view of city, horizon, and sky. The air seemed different up here. But we had entered Althaus's world, and it was vast and exhilarating.

Bratke walked up to a large painting. "Didn't that disappear when Hitler and Goebbels cleansed out the so-called degenerate in German art?"

Althaus waved us to matching Mies van der Rohe armchairs.

"Correct. But clearly not forever. Now, my gentlemen, I am going to give you a brandy from the late Führer's Chancellery that was supposedly completely consumed by either the SS or the Soviets in April 1945."

It was as if we were powerless to resist. In his high airy room, Althaus was master. I glanced at Bratke. He seemed to be taking everything in his stride. Althaus disappeared into another room.

"I'm going to enjoy all this until I find a concrete reason not to," Bratke whispered. "So we are all right for at least another thirty seconds! Seriously, Steve, I don't think we're in actual danger."

"He must be crazy."

Bratke shook his head.

"No, I don't think so. But he has something he must say, and to me. And he will be hospitable in the process. You don't survive and prosper like this only by mere physical violence."

Althaus came back into the room, carrying a silver tray and three large glasses. The glasses each had a couple of inches of brandy in them—the rich heady aroma was already invading the fresh air.

"Come."

He handed out the glasses.

"Your health, my gentlemen! Mr. Bratke and my young man Mr. McDowell."

The brandy was gorgeous. It was invasive. Up so high above the ground, the ordinary city streets, it seemed to symbolise release from the everyday world. Release into what, was another question.

Eventually Althaus spoke again. "My dear Mr. Bratke, it is not every day that I make a request of someone. I have done that maybe four times in sixty years. But I grow old, and I lose my inhibitions, and even some of my most regular habits." He sipped at his brandy, and a smirk came to his lips. "So I have decided to ask of you a favour, Mr. Bratke, and what I feel is a very great one."

"All right. I'll listen. But why?" Bratke said. "And why me?"

"You are a remarkable man," Althaus replied. "I have met with many remarkable men, but I know that you are very different. Mr. Bratke, I grow old, and even I know that I will not live forever. I have done many things that I should not have done. If I were a Christian perhaps I should say that I have sinned. I would say that what I require now is absolution, Mr. Bratke. The taking away of my sins."

Bratke seemed unsurprised. "Dr. Althaus, you need to confess before you can receive absolution. You need a priest." He sipped his brandy. "Or a direct line to God, or whatever god you believe in."

Althaus laughed, and slapped his hand down on his knee. "Exactly! Mr. Bratke, you will hear my confession, as it were. Mr. McDowell will be our witness. I believe in no god except me. I will have no other gods except me. But I do not wish to be my own priest. I know you are a remarkable fellow, Mr. Bratke. Come, my dear sir, I know about everything and everyone that you have ever been involved with in Germany. Oh, and everywhere else, too. Back home, for example. I believe it all, let me tell you. I believe now. You can listen. Then you can take my past away from me. You can free me."

I think that my mouth was gaping wider and wider as Althaus spoke. Bratke flashed me a glance and I came back to myself. I took a swig of the brandy. I had been watching King Herod lobbying for a job in a maternity ward.

"You come from the land of the seven fortresses, from the back end of beyond, my dear Bratke," Althaus said. "And you know as well as I do that good walls make good neighbours. But one can, if one wishes and is able to, look out and past them, as well as cultivating that which lies within. Yes, I know. Not so, eh?"

Bratke sat there. I felt the great winds of the upper air come and go through the bright room. Bratke just sat there. Then he nodded slowly. In a voice that he tried to keep as non-committal as he could, he said: "So, then. Exactly what is it that you want to tell me, Dr. Althaus?"

❧

Althaus sat back in his chair.

"I need to tell you the main story of my life. Also the story of someone else." He looked at me. "I have heard you out at work, Mr. McDowell. You are very good. You know your history. I think that even a young man such as you, who was not alive when the events that I am going to describe took place, will understand and see in a different light some of the reasons why I acted as I did. I also know that Mr. Bratke is no fool, and very deeply informed. He has been touched to the heart in many things. But you will be a bonus here, Mr. McDowell, because we do have at least one thing in common. And it is important."

"I don't know what you mean."

"You will." Althaus smiled tightly. "You see, Mr. McDowell, and you know, of course, that Berlin has long had a reputation for the toleration of, ah, alternative lifestyles. During the time of the Weimar Republic, Berlin was almost notorious. Why, when I was a young child, I saw your Mr. Isherwood himself on one occasion. I knew even from that early age. Even after the National Socialist Fascists came to power, it was not wiped out entirely. After it proved necessary to construct the Anti-Fascist Protection Barrier, Berlin had two—"

What Althaus was saying dawned on me.

"Ah, I see that you now understand. Of course, not even I could never have declared myself."

"Is this all that you wanted to say, Dr. Althaus?" Bratke asked.

"No, of course it is not," he snapped. "My story is more important than that. But I have adapted enough to realise that who I am is an important part of why things happened the way they did, the way I made them happen. It was inevitable, perhaps, but not only because of my own nature.

"I will continue. I only wanted you to know."

I knew that I'd have to be even more careful. Now Althaus had showed that he could be disarmingly honest, as well, it would be all too easy to take anything that he said at face value. I was glad that it was Matthias Bratke that Althaus really wanted to talk to. I was sure that Bratke's discernment was better than mine, his defences stronger.

"Very well, my gentlemen," Althaus said. "I was born here, in Berlin-Friedrichshain, not so very far from where we are now. The street is no longer there. The whole area was very badly bombed, and after a few years the remaining buildings were removed. That part of my young life has been obliterated. My parents were Social Democrats, but my Uncle Karl was a dedicated Communist. My father had been arrested when Hitler came to power, and that experience scared both my parents, as well as having physically injured my father. My parents became enthusiastic National Socialists. Uncle Karl understood, but he took it upon himself to educate me politically.

"You see, he was a good actor. Outwardly he became a better Hitlerite than even Horst Wessel himself had been. But with my parents it was a conversion of convenience that became genuine conviction. With my uncle it was a conversion made out of pure cynicism and self-interest. He had been one of the members of the Communist Party of Germany who had hated the Weimar Republic as much as the Nazis had done. And he knew it. And I caught on young.

"When that champagne salesman, the supposed 'von' Ribbentrop, signed the Non-Aggression Pact with Stalin, Uncle Karl stayed put. That was just as well, because many surviving Communists were betrayed by the NKVD to the Gestapo. My uncle was not one of them. He said to me, 'Never forget that the facts are what those with the guns, cameras, and printing presses want them to be. Those people will stamp on faces for generations, any faces, for many generations. We must do anything to avoid being stamped on, even if it means doing the stamping ourselves. Never forget that.' I never did.

"I grew up to young adulthood during the war. My deluded parents were killed in one of the early air raids of the Battle of Berlin. They died as proper and correct Nazis, thinking that Uncle Karl had betrayed his old Socialism even more than they had, or their party had done. But I knew. How could I not, as he took me into his confidence?

"I had become an enthusiastic member of the Hitler Youth. Don't misunderstand me, my gentlemen—there was no choice, but I embraced it. A few lads around my age managed to evade membership, but things never went easy for them. As the air raids continued, more and more of the city was reduced to ruin. Life became more and more circumscribed. Goebbels's propaganda was incessant. Uncle Karl actually rather admired that poisonous dwarf. He told me that it had been a major error to let him get away from our side. But we Communists had never been quite lucky enough to have had our own Hitler.

"By 1945 most of us knew the truth, what would happen in no more than a few months' time at most. Berlin, if not most of Germany, would be overrun by the Russians, and our world really would end, in the blood and flames of the *Götterdämmerung* of Hitler and his courtiers. Part of me rejoiced in that. Uncle Karl had often talked of the new world that could be forged out of the old. He had read the forbidden authors such as your Mr. H.G. Wells, and many of Wells's dreams had become mine. Such dreams were the only dreams that I allowed myself.

"Yet I was, and am, enough of a German and a realist to find that total destruction was repugnant. I was young, but I knew that I wanted there still to be a Germany for me, in my lifetime. I wasn't worried about other people, but I wanted a country for me. Also, I had fallen in love."

Althaus smiled his tight-lipped smile again. He got up and took our brandy glasses away. A moment later, he returned with them filled, and the bottle.

"Yes, I was in love," he continued. "His name was Thomas. He was a year or so older than me, and was one of the local Hitler Youth activists. Like me, he was also leading something of a hidden life, even at that age. Thomas felt the same way about me, although I was not his first. Thomas was a fine lad, a true Aryan, and he was really the only reason that made me stay in Berlin during those last few months of the war.

"Of course, escape would have been extremely dangerous. By then there were many special squads. People who were suspected of being defeatist or subversive, or who were in the wrong place at the wrong time with no adequate reason, soldiers or civilians, were often executed out of hand, and their bodies left out on the street.

"But for a few weeks little of these sort of events mattered to me. Thomas and I spent every moment we could together, as well as on Hitler Youth activities. To everyone, he seemed to be the perfect young leader, an example to live up to. I was his loyal and willing lieutenant in more ways than they could know. Goebbels should have had a film made about Thomas.

"I did not see so much of my uncle by then, even though I was still living in his apartment. He still cynically regarded my activities as inescapable. He still looked for the new dawn that he believed was approaching from the east, as the Russians approached Berlin.

"Then one day Thomas shocked me. We were lying in his bed, and talking about the coming defence of the city. He told me that because most of the older men had been called up into the army, or the laughable Home Guard militia, it would be up to the loyal Hitler Youth like us to defend Berlin, to the end if necessary. I made all the right responses. Then Thomas said our squad was going to be sent to barracks not far from Charlottenburg Palace for more training."

While Althaus had been talking, he had been looking past us, out of the window. Now he looked directly at us.

"Well, do you know that area?"

We both nodded.

"Sure," I said. "It's about half-way out to Spandau. There was a lot of heavy fighting round there. The Palace itself was very badly damaged."

"Once again you are correct, Mr. McDowell. Well, we were sent there two or three days later. We were a group of young schoolboys, fifteen, sixteen years of age. Some of us were willing to do anything, to kill cowards, traitors, Russians—even to die."

"You weren't frightened, Dr. Althaus?" Bratke broke in.

"Some of us lads were most certainly not." Althaus replied. "I thought that Thomas was one who wanted to fight to the end, and that is what frightened and shocked me. That I would lose him, or be killed and he would be left alive to find someone else, for someone else to have him.

"During our first night in the barracks, Thomas got into my bed and held me tightly. He was very tender. He shocked me again. He told me that he was going to desert, to get out of the city and travel westwards, and surrender to the Americans or the British, on the other side of the Elbe. He was getting help, false papers, from one of the barracks guards. Thomas had been bribing him. He did not go into details. Thomas told me that he had relatives in Hamburg, and if he could get to them, things would be all right.

"I was shattered. I tried not to cry. Then, a moment later, I was so disgusted with myself for having allowed myself to fall under Thomas's spell for so long, when he was going to abandon me. I realised that I had allowed myself to grow weak, and that I had been trusting someone. That had done me no good at all.

"Thomas asked me to promise that I would not say anything. I agreed. When he finally left me alone, I still could not sleep, and I lay there thinking. The Russians were shelling the eastern parts of the city by then, and even in Charlottenburg the night was punctuated by the noise of the explosions, and the flashes of light. It was often quite deafening.

"The next morning, as we were marched off for the day's training, Thomas kept glancing at me. I wondered if he realised that he had put his life into my hands by telling me what he was planning to do. On the far edge of the parade-ground we were suddenly ordered to halt, and form up into ranks. One of the real fanatics, a short dark boy called Werner, shouted a short speech at us. He yelled that here was an opportunity not to be missed. We were going to watch what happened to deserters and cowards. Then we saw three boys being led out from the cell-block. They must have been fifteen or sixteen. Kids. Two of them were crying. They were stood against the wall, and shot. It was as quick and simple as that. Then we were marched off again. Thomas did not look at me again for the rest of the day.

"Back at the barracks, as we were queuing to receive our rations, Thomas said that there was going to be another execution shortly, a Home Guard man who had turned out to be a secret Communist. He had been ordered to be one of the witnesses to it, and then he was going to have to take some messages to the command post in Spandau. He was then going to go absent without leave, as he had told me. Thomas asked me to come with him. There was only his one set of false papers, but we would get through because of all the confusion. We would be able to mingle with refugees fleeing westwards from the Russians. There would be lots of soldiers separated from their units. He said that we would both be safe if only we could get to the other side of the Elbe.

"I thought fast. Of course I said that I would go with him. If that had been the first time that he had mentioned it, I think that I would have thrown myself into his arms, even in front of all our comrades. But I had had second thoughts about Thomas. Love can vanish so quickly. Eh, Mr. McDowell? Mr. Bratke?"

"Just carry on," Bratke said quietly. He pursed his lips.

"After we had eaten all the rations they would give us, Thomas and I and several other lads were ordered out into a courtyard to watch this next execution. I remember it clearly. 'How could any Bolshevik have survived for so long?' one of the lads said. 'He has to die, so that we can live,' another said. We were lined up. There was a noose hanging from one of the tall lampposts that lit up the courtyard. So this was going to be a hanging. Werner stood beside me. 'No use in wasting bullets on him,' he whispered. 'Look, here he comes now.'

"A middle-aged man was walking between two SS men. The SS were dressed in their black uniforms—not immaculate any more but still much more so than any of the soldiers that I had seen for weeks. The man between them was in shabby and dirty civilian clothes. He looked wildly around him as they led him to the lamppost and pushed him up onto the chair that was ready and waiting. The noose was put around his neck.

"Gentlemen, it was my Uncle Karl."

Neither Bratke nor I moved or said anything. I didn't know whether or not Althaus was expecting either of us to ask a question, to ask how he'd felt, or anything like that. It didn't seem that Bratke was going to assist Althaus with his story, or allow him any further self-justification of any kind.

Althaus cleared his throat.

"I do not know if he saw me or not. For a moment I thought he was looking straight at me. But he didn't move or shout out. There was no sign of recognition. And I thought that I should say something. But not for long. How would I have explained that I knew this man, let alone was related to him? At that moment, whether or not he knew me, I did not know him. It was impossible. It would have been my death-warrant as well. My uncle was standing in my way, and was just about to be removed. I could not allow myself to think otherwise. One of the Hitler Youth fanatics handed one of the SS men a placard, which he put around the Communist's neck. It said, 'I am an enemy of the Fatherland. I deserve to die'. Then the chair was kicked away. Uncle Karl swung around, convulsing and gasping. Eventually he became still, and just gently swung there, rotating slowly. 'Leave him there,' one of the SS men said.

"On our way to our quarters, Thomas said that we would be leaving shortly. He had been given the satchel with the messages to take to Spandau in it, and had collected his false papers earlier. His secret was still safe with anyone who knew it.

"At the main gate, Thomas grinned at the guard. 'I need Althaus here to come with me. It is all right.' I smiled as well, but I could never be as winning as Thomas was able to be. The guard and Thomas exchanged a few words that I did not make out. Then we were walking away from the barracks.

"Thomas told me that there had been no spare bicycles, or he would have got us a couple. There were no buses or trams either. Luckily it was only about six or seven kilometres to Spandau—but we would never arrive there. Thomas said that he had planned for us to turn south and head out of Berlin along the Heerstrasse—at least, after it had got dark. It was beginning to get dark now, but the skies behind us, from the north round to the south, were lit up by explosions and fires apparently burning out of control. We both knew that the war was lost, Germany was lost, the city was lost.

"But I was not going to be lost.

"We hurried along the pavements, not talking or looking at anyone we passed. In any case there were very few people around. Everyone was hiding in their cellars or in the air-raid shelters. Most shops had long since been closed for business. Occasionally an army truck drove past, and we got out of the way. We could still prove we were going to Spandau if we were challenged, but the last thing that we wanted was to perhaps be given a lift to right where we did not want to go.

"Explosions rocked the city every few seconds. I wanted to get out as quickly as possible. When we had got past Westend, Thomas said that he needed to make a decision. 'We must turn off and head south now, or continue almost into Spandau itself. Theo, whatever we do, we have to avoid the Olympic Stadium. I know that we're going to be concentrating forces there against the Russian attack.' Thomas laughed for a moment, a quick bitter laugh. 'Our forces are mere Hitler Youth. That's about all that's left round here. Us and Home Guard old men. We mustn't get caught up with any units being sent to the Stadium.'

"He decided that we would continue along the Spandauer Damm, and head off to the south a little way past Ruhleben. We would be able to travel to the west of the Olympic Stadium complex during the night. Also there were a lot of gardens and allotments there, so there would be plenty of cover for us.

"We continued along the street, keeping close to the inside of the pavement, hugging close to blocks of flats and walls, and running quickly past open spaces like roads and bomb sites. Once or twice, as we ran, I looked behind me. I saw the Radio Tower silhouetted against livid and flaming clouds. There were flashes and a constant sound like thunder.

"Thomas knew his Berlin. I had to give him that. Eventually we stopped at a street corner, near the Spandau boundary. He pointed down the street and said: 'We must turn off down there. If we're stopped now, we'll probably be shot as deserters and traitors.' Stumbling over rubble and broken glass, we darted into a shop doorway. We rested for a few minutes, and we shared out the bits of our rations that we had been able to save. Thomas put his arms around me and kissed me. It was like the old times for us. I responded. He whispered that we would both be safe in Hamburg. Then I remembered that there was only the one set of false papers, and that Thomas had them for himself. So I kept myself back again.

"We walked on fast down the street. We tried to look as if we were going somewhere definite, that we were clearly walking with a definite aim. Thomas kept one hand firmly on the satchel slung over his shoulder. Luckily we had still not met anyone, or seen anyone who had taken any notice of us. Hopefully we just looked like two lads out on an important mission, and it would not be worth anyone's time and effort to stop or challenge us. We headed southwest, leaving Spandau to the north. We were in a very suburban area. Then Thomas whispered to me, 'There's a small bridge across the Havel up ahead. We have to cross it. It will probably be guarded. Theo, I don't want to have to swim if I can help it. If we're stopped, we'll have to take our chances, maybe say that we got lost, or that we had to take a detour on our way to Spandau.'

"Soon the bridge came into view. It was almost completely dark now. There were no streetlights, and if there were any other lights, they were all hidden in the blackout.

There was just the constant subdued roaring from the city behind us, the white and yellow flashes in the sky, and the dull red glow of our hell over everything.

"Then we reached the bridge. There were two old men with old-fashioned rifles guarding it. One of them ordered us to stop. The other pointed his rifle at us, moving it from Thomas to me, and back again, like he was uncertain of which of us was the greatest threat, or the gun was too heavy for him, and he had to keep shifting its weight to avoid dropping it. Thomas whispered that he would do the talking.

" 'Good evening, sirs, we must get to Headquarters in Spandau.'

" 'You're well out of your way, boys,' said the man who had stopped us. 'Why are you going to Spandau? You must be needed in the city centre.'

"Thomas patted the satchel. 'We are based at Charlottenburg. We are following our orders. We have despatches to take to Headquarters in Spandau.'

" 'Let me see.'

" 'This bag is for Colonel Beckmann only. You must let us pass. We had to come this way, you must not delay us.'

"The other man spoke then. 'Let the lads through, Hans. You couldn't see anything anyway.'

" 'We have our orders, Gerold. No-one is to cross the bridge out of the city except for the best of reasons. These boys don't convince me.' He slung his rifle and held his hand out. 'Let's see your papers.' He squinted at me. 'Do you speak?'

" 'Leave him alone,' Thomas said. 'He is under my command.'

"The other man laughed. 'My son's like you, he's still young, thinks he runs the whole place.' He paused. 'Last I heard from him he was still in Königsberg. Come on, let them through, Hans. It can't make any difference now. I tell you, I'm heading for home soon. I had to leave my wife by herself with our grandchildren. I'll be more use there, from what I've heard about the Russians.' He slammed the butt of his rifle down on the ground, holding it like he was on parade. He was staying out of it.

"I saw that the two men were under tremendous tension. Well, who was not, in those days? But these were not regular soldiers. They seemed old enough to have served in the 1914-18 war, and might have been on the old side even then. Gerold certainly did not want to be outside in the shell-fire, defending a bridge in some godforsaken suburb. Hans was stronger. No doubt both had been sincere supporters of the regime—it was men like that who had benefited from it. Now it was the militia for both of them. Gerold was losing heart. We could forget him. It seemed to me that Hans was still dangerous. Some people go on acting until the very end, even if what they have believed in has been taken away, destroyed, or exposed as false and pointless. People like that can do so much damage, taking others down with them.

" 'All right, boys, let me check the satchel and you can cross.' Maybe he thought we had food or cigarettes in it. Hans held out his hand again, while he began to unsling his rifle. He seemed to have forgotten that no-one was covering us. Thomas started to fiddle with the strap of the satchel. Hans came up to me. 'Let me have a look at you too, silent boy.' He put his hand under my chin, and lifted my head up a little. I stepped back slightly. 'Don't move,' he said. There was little light, except from the explosions and fires. Then he moved his hand up and pushed my helmet back slightly. It had always been too big for me. A flash of light illuminated our faces. Hans said, 'Sweet. I think. Now, boys—'

" 'For God's sake, Hans!' Gerold shouted.

" 'Run!' Thomas shouted. He side-swiped Hans with the satchel as he dodged past him, and ran on over the bridge. I shook off Hans's arm, and started running as well. I heard laughter. I glanced back. In the gloom I saw that Gerold was still standing there, upright with his rifle like a sentry on parade. Hans was pointing his rifle at us.

"He fired twice. He missed us. It did not seem that he was going to chase after us. We ran on, along the dark street. The houses grew further apart. I outran Thomas, and then waited while he caught up with me.

" 'Let's stop, Theo. Please. Please.'

"He had not said 'please' to me like that since our last good night together. We slumped down on the kerb. Thomas put his hand on my knee. Then I realised that the guard had not missed us after all. I was getting covered in Thomas's blood.

"Thomas unslung the satchel and put it on the ground. I listened for the sound of anyone running after us, but I heard nothing except for the rumbling of explosions. Thomas said, 'Please let's just stop for a moment, I'll be all right . . . '

"I said that he knew we could not stop. We had to keep moving. He had said that himself. I put my hand on the satchel. Thomas looked at me. I saw his face in the dull red of the cloudy sky. He was frightened—the first time I had really seen him scared. Tears leaked out of his eyes and trickled slowly down his dusty cheeks.

" 'Theo, I'll be all right,' he said. 'Please don't go.' Then for a moment a crafty look came into his eyes. Once more I had been wavering. I had been about to say that we could rest for five more minutes. I was about to put my arm around his shoulder, and wipe his tears away. But I remembered that he had been about to betray me. I hardened my heart. 'Listen, Theo, we must stay together, I'm the only one who knows where we have to cross the Elbe to be safe. In Hamburg they're my relatives, not yours . . . '

"I moved the satchel away from him. Thomas tried to get up, but he could hardly move. He must have been losing blood fast. He was getting weaker. 'I'm leaving in two minutes,' I told him. 'Whether you can travel or not.' I stood up and grabbed hold of the bag and slung it over my shoulder. It was heavier than I expected. I undid the flap and felt around inside. There were some documents, a paper bag with what felt like a bread roll in it—and a pistol.

"Thomas knew that I had found it. 'Don't,' he said. Then he started to cry: great heaving sobs. I told him to keep quiet, and that I would not hurt him. 'You can't leave me, you can't,' he wailed. But his voice was getting quieter. I looked down at the pavement. There was a huge dark patch there. Thomas' life-blood. I was really seeing blood spilling for the Fatherland.

"Well, none of it was ever going to be mine if I could help it. That moment was another turning-point for me. I looked up and down the dark road, and then back down at Thomas. He made another attempt to move, but gave it up. Then he fell back against the cobbles. I crouched down, keeping the satchel well out of the way. I thought that he could be playing a trick, despite the fact that he'd lost so much blood. I was never going to trust him anymore. For all his beauty, his smile, the ways he'd had with me, I was never going to trust him.

"I just crouched there for a few moments. Thomas did not move. I knelt, and leant in closer. I didn't think that he was breathing anymore. He must have finally bled to death. There was one good thought: that I would not have to finish him off myself. Because, my gentlemen, I would have done it. I had been thinking about how I should do it, that if it could only be one of us who would get away and survive it was going to be me and not him. I went through his pockets, and found the identity papers. There were two sets: one made out under a false name for him, and another made out for me.

"I wasted valuable time shouting at him, the dead Thomas. How dare he put me to all this trouble? If he had wanted to surprise me with a loving gesture, there were other ways to do that, not by making me think that he held an advantage, and then showing me that we were equal. He really did love me. And I hated him and felt all the more contempt because he had let me win by not being strong enough to show it when it might have saved him. Instead, he was weak, he was not living in the world where we found ourselves. He had acted by the old rules. I detest that.

"I got up and left him. Of course, I had absolutely no intention whatsoever of leaving Berlin and trying to cross the Elbe and surrender to the Americans or the British. I was not going to look for Thomas's relatives in Hamburg, either. Germany was going to be full of refugees, boys my age on the move. I had papers and a gun. We were approaching Zero Hour. After Zero Hour is the First Hour."

Althaus stopped talking. I came to myself again, wrenched away from the inferno of Berlin in April 1945. The clean and airy white room seemed like somewhere on another planet. Beyond the windows, the sky was still there, untroubled. Bratke finished his brandy, and I took an expensive mouthful of mine. It burnt my throat, before exploding into comfortable warmth. But I still shivered with the sensation.

"Do you want to continue?" Bratke said.

"You are so much like a pastor!" Althaus replied. "But you for one are not weak!"

"So, what now, Dr. Althaus?"

"Very well. I survived through Zero Hour. Yes, you know that. I survived everything Berlin and the Allies threw at me. The false identity that Thomas had got for me came with a history—one I made up myself. Hitler Youth fanatic, fascist of fascists. I would have joined the National Socialist German Workers' Party as soon as I'd been old enough. I always called the Party by its full name. I went through de-Nazification. That was one thing that I used the British for. Their way was the most decent, you would say, perhaps, Mr. McDowell? Here was a young and impressionable German lad, with a mind still to be fully formed . . . I was good-looking then, as well. But as if you could change the very grooves along which my mind already moved! I came out pronounced cured, don't you know?

"I used my imagination, and I used my gun when I needed to. I used all of my resources. There really was such a small leap, in so many ways, from joining the Nazi Party to wanting to join the Socialist Unity Party. Communist of communists, it was so easy. The Stasi as well. Totalitarianism is all the same, really, if you are a man in the street. That is why it was necessary that I made myself a good place within its structure. I was not the only one to move over. I tell you, my gentlemen, for all that I am saying I could have worked my way up in the machinery of the Federal Republic's bureaucracy and so-called democracy. Whatever I was, whatever I did, I did not go through the mental gymnastics that some that fled to the West did. I stayed honest to myself, in my own way. I have always prided myself in my realism.

"I think that I would have been one of those men whom you would call an *éminence grise*, or a worker in the 'backroom'. I rose within the SED, but I did not hold any position that made me well-known."

Althaus waved towards a row of small black-and-white photos, framed on the wall next to the kitchen door. They were too small to make out individually, but I'd seen that they looked like faces.

"They were our leaders, the great men. Pieck, Ulbricht, Grotewohl, Mielke, Honecker, and all the others. They had the photos, the films, and the newsreels. I kept in the background. I was never elected to anything. I never stood on a platform reviewing troops, I never visited farmers in the fields, or addressed the People's Chamber. I served the people in other ways. Hardly anyone knew my face. Hardly anyone knew where I lived. True, I had my personal needs, but only a few. The DDR's laws regarding people like us, Mr. McDowell, were more human than those of that so-called Federal Republic. And money? Do you see evidence of its misuse around here?"

Althaus stopped talking, and sipped his brandy.

"My gentlemen, let me say just this. I was the German Democratic Republic. That is all I claim. I have told you all that I said I would, and you have listened. You have kept your side of the bargain so far. Now, Mr. Bratke, I require you to complete our little agreement. Take it all away."

I finished my brandy, and looked around the room. I deliberately avoided looking at Bratke and Theodor Althaus. I didn't want to catch the eyes of either of them. In fact, if I could've become invisible, I would've done. What was going to follow was going to have to be between them only. I looked around the room. Then I got up and walked across to the row of photographs. I pretended to study them carefully, and to be utterly absorbed. Actually, I was utterly absorbed. I gazed at each portrait in turn, almost hypnotised by the gaze of each man. Maybe it had been the brandy doing it. But I found myself almost wishing to enter into their worlds, and what it had been that had driven them, made them what they were, and contributed to what they had done. Perhaps their hearts had been in the right place. Or perhaps they had been merely opportunistic hypocritical cynics, like Althaus had made himself out to be by telling us his own story.

Neither Althaus nor Bratke spoke. I stood with my back to them. I tried to sink into the background, but at the same time I kept my ears open. I wondered what Bratke would do next. Would the airy high room become a sort of confessional in the sky? With Bratke going about his priest-like task, and telling the penitent Althaus that his sins were forgiven and that he could go in peace, but must sin no more?

"Mr. Bratke, I do not have all night," Althaus said eventually.

"Dr. Althaus, you have as long as you have," Bratke snapped. "You are treating me like some sort of mediaeval priest or witch-doctor. You want to confess and then receive your forgiveness, like it's a simple mechanical operation. I have listened. My friend Mr. McDowell has listened too. I can afford to listen. I suspect that Mr. McDowell would be better employed out on the street looking for business. Right now I need to think."

Althaus laughed, a harsh cackle. I smiled at what Bratke had said—or rather, the words he had used to say it. I knew what he'd meant.

"He would not have been long on the street if I had been younger," Althaus said. "Why, he is still a lovely young man. They all—"

I turned round. "You old bastard," I shouted. "You used me to set up all this." I waved my arms at the room, the window, the rushing sky outside the windows. "Okay, okay, that's all right, I've been used, and I've been used to it. But not by a fucking dried-up old relic like you. Just because you've always had your price. If you ever knew love or just being close to someone, you lost it a long time ago. Or threw it away, more like. Don't judge me by your standards."

I sat back down again. "I'm sorry," I said, but while only looking at Bratke. I didn't want to complicate things for him.

Bratke smiled. There was peace and calm in that smile, and he meant it to be just for me. There was no patronising, no false pity or false sympathy. Only an urbane, human contact.

Althaus laughed again, but it was a quiet, resigned laugh.

"The human comedy still fascinates me. Mr. McDowell, of course I have been spoken to like that before. The young men have often even survived. I do judge you by my standards, because my standards rule. I am like your Mr. Disraeli, when it was said of him that he was a self-made man who worships his creator. At Zero Hour I became a creator, I made myself and the world I moved in. My creed is that I have no other gods but me. But—but—I am dying. That is what it is all about, gentlemen. The human comedy has won, and I will not be observing it for much longer.

"Mr. Bratke, do what you promised, take it all from me. Here I am god, but I am no physician. I cannot heal myself."

"I cannot forgive you, Dr. Althaus," Bratke said quietly.

Althaus stared at Bratke, and then turned his gaze on me. He knew I was the weaker of the two. Defiance, power, and hate poured out of that face. I couldn't help but think that he really would soon be dead at that rate.

"I cannot be the one to forgive you, Dr. Althaus, but I will do what you asked. If you would but only let me."

Now I wondered if Bratke was going to turn into some sort of preacher. He would be producing a Bible and issuing an altar-call any moment.

"I have told you my story. What more is there?"

"There is one word that you can say."

"Which is?"

"You know it. It's a word that I doubt you've spoken in sixty years. Or at least, as if you really meant it."

Althaus stared straight ahead.

"Tell me, what is this word?"

Bratke got up and walked over to where Althaus was sitting. Slowly, carefully, he knelt down next to him.

"Dr. Althaus. Theodor. Theo."

"Yes."

"Here."

Bratke put his hand on Althaus's shoulder. The tenderness was obvious. I knew it, from when Markus touched me like that . . . Bratke leant close in to Althaus and whispered in his ear. He stayed in that position for several seconds, maybe even ten or twenty. He whispered again. Then he got up and walked back to his chair.

"Get the brandy, please, Steve," Bratke said.

❧

We were sitting in Jens's Café.

"No, I won't tell you what I said to him," Bratke said. "Anyway, you should be able to work it out for yourself. It's obvious. A child would know. But—I suppose that Althaus never really was a child. He never really got the chance."

"Millions of boys and girls his age lost their childhoods," I said. "Not everyone turned out like him."

"He seemed to have had a run of special opportunities, and maybe he has been more honest than most. Although in his case it is hardly a virtue."

Jens brought over two more coffees. And a small bottle of clear spirit. He grinned as he left it on the table between us.

165

"Althaus had a good line in quotations from English politicians," Bratke said. "There is another good one. Stanley Baldwin said it. Something like this: 'Dictatorship is like a beech tree—very magnificent to look at, but nothing grows underneath it.'

"It's simple, Steve. There's nothing there, not any more, anyway. Althaus is nothing. He thought he was god. He certainly exercised that sort of power. But he became nothing, empty. And what is more powerless or pitiful than a god whom no-one worships any more, one whom time has deposed?"

"How did you free him then?"

"I spoke a few words, and told him what to do with one of them. The important one. That was enough to free him. He is free now, for all I know. But I won't be staying in Berlin long enough to find out."

"You're leaving? But we've—"

"It's all right, Steve, it really is. If Althaus should contact you again, you will be able to reach me, I promise, should you need to. And we have not seen the last of each other. For a start I've not properly met your Markus yet, and I know I'll do that.

"But did I free Theodor Althaus? Well . . . "

Bratke poured some of the spirit into each of our coffees. We raised our cups.

"Your health! Now. Althaus wanted to be freed of something he thought that he carried with him, and could give away to someone willing to receive it, to take it off him. Well, that's okay. But he really had to want to give it up. Maybe he didn't really want to. I haven't taken or received anything. He thinks that I have, but I haven't. I ought to know. He thinks he's given me it all. But he hasn't.

"Dr. Theodor Althaus will die soon, as stunted and half-formed as any dictatorship is, whatever its outward power and glory. That's also why religion is of no use to him, any more than it was to me in our transaction. Religion has the same faults as dictatorship, except that you can't see the non-existent god that you're creating in your own image. And any system that tries to teach that one and one is three has nothing to offer, in the long run. Really, Steve."

I nodded. I'd worked all that out for myself long ago.

"So what was that word, Matthias?"

"Steve, you're impossible!"

While Jens laughed, Matthias Bratke leant over the table and whispered it to me. Yes, it was simple and obvious. And then, as I was laughing too, Markus came in through the door.

"So where is my drink then?" he demanded with a grin, before joining in our laughter.

Sometimes Markus and I still have a laugh when we remember that evening in Jens's Café. We hold each other, and then I think of the high bright room above the Leipziger Strasse, and what happened there, and what Althaus brought to life there.

It's often on my mind.

But not too much.

Because I have the word, and know that I can use it.

Acknowledgements

The publisher and author would like to thank
Meggan Kehrli for her cover and design,
Eoin Llewellyn for the use of his painting,
Jim Rockhill for his proofreading,
Ken Mackenzie for typesetting this book,
and Joe Mitchen for his continuing support.

The Silver Voices
was first published in Bucharest, Romania
by Ex Occidente Press in May 2010.

About the Author

John Howard was born in London. His books include *The Silver Voices*, *Written by Daylight*, *Buried Shadows*, *A Flowering Wound*, and *The Voice of the Air*. With Mark Valentine has written the joint collections *Secret Europe, Inner Europe, Powers and Presences*, and *This World and That Other*. His stories have appeared in many anthologies. He has published essays on various aspects of the science fiction and horror fields, including such iconic authors as Fritz Leiber, Arthur Machen, and August Derleth. He has also written about many now lesser-known and unfairly obscure authors and their work.

SWAN RIVER PRESS

Founded in 2003, Swan River Press is an independent publishing company, based in Dublin, Ireland, dedicated to gothic, supernatural, and fantastic literature. We specialise in limited edition hardbacks, publishing fiction from around the world with an emphasis on Ireland's contributions to the genre.

www.swanriverpress.ie

*"Handsome, beautifully made volumes . . .
altogether irresistible."*

– Michael Dirda, *Washington Post*

*"It [is] often down to small, independent, specialist presses
to keep the candle of horror fiction flickering . . . "*

– Darryl Jones, *Irish Times*

*"Swan River Press has emerged as one of the most inspiring
new presses over the past decade. Not only are the books
beautifully presented and professionally produced, but they
aspire consistently to high literary quality and originality,
ranging from current writers of supernatural/weird fiction
to rare or forgotten works by departed authors."*

– Peter Bell, *Ghosts & Scholars*

WRITTEN BY DAYLIGHT

John Howard

Sunsets in a London suburb, and a transformation into an Earthly paradise; paths winding through a Transylvanian palace gardens, and an obsessed journey towards a Mediterranean dream; a city so ancient that even its total disappearance has been forgotten, and an island of shifting sands that can never be truly mapped . . . The vivid and diverse settings of these stories are façades obscuring reality for the exiles and outcasts who find their way into them. Seemingly born out of time and place, they seek the right routes to bring them to where they want to be, but there are many diversions on the way. In these stories of haunted landscapes and intimidating cities many possibilities confront the unwary, but there is usually only one choice to be made.

"Howard's work is both delicate and powerful."

– The Agony Column

*"If there is a unifying theme here it is the transience
of existence, from the individual to the social
and even the geographical . . . not only well-written
but also offer remarkable ideas."*

– Supernatural Tales

*"Most of these tales are so subtle as to defy
any category of the strange at all, but reward
re-reading and are all the greater for it."*

– The Pan Review

A FLOWERING WOUND

John Howard

Two of the stories in this collection by John Howard have their setting in a certain west London suburb—the calm prospect of its small houses and tree-lined roads is deceptive. And throughout this selection of stories, whether in outer London or hyperinflationary Berlin, Romania in the febrile 1930s, or the austerity Britain of recent years, we encounter people who live on the peripheries of their cities and societies—and at the edge of their own lives and illusions. They might think they know the rules, but it often turns out they do not, after all. Or perhaps the rules changed—silently, abruptly. In these stories past and present come together with wounding consequences for those caught out by the system—or its absence.

"Some stories recall Arthur Machen's approach to London, his insistence that the great metropolis is a place of magic and mystery."

– Supernatural Tales

"Full of haunting stories of love and confusion . . . a very suitable accompaniment to these terrifying times."

– A Ghostly Company

SELECTED STORIES

Mark Valentine

In St. Petersburg, amidst an uneasy truce with the revolution, there exists a secret trade in looted ikons. But who are the dark strangers seeking for the Gate of the Archangel? In the small town of Tzern, news arrives of the death of the Emperor; meanwhile a postmaster, a priest, a prophet and a war-wearied soldier watch the dawn for signs of the future. Constantinople: A quest for the lost faiths of the former Ottoman Empire leads a French scholar to believe that the strangest may also be the truest. On the edges of Europe, exiles and idealists meet in a café to talk of their hopes—while sinister forces begin to march. These stories, exquisitely told by Mark Valentine, are about individuals caught up in the endings of old empires—and of what comes next.

"Dense, allusive, and thoroughly satisfying."

– Dead Reckonings

"[These stories] are all imbued with a strangeness and beauty that takes them—and the reader— several removes from what is called realism."

– Supernatural Tales

"Valentine is a master at capturing the ineffable in prose."

– The Agony Column

www.ingramcontent.com/pod-product-compliance
Lightning Source LLC
Chambersburg PA
CBHW030956210726
48290CB00007B/2332